A HONEYMOON IN SPACE

GEORGE GRIFFITH

Illustrated by Stanley L. Wood

Apogee Science Fiction

A Honeymoon in Space
First published in 1900
Originally serialized
in a slightly different form as
Stories of Other Worlds in
Pearson's Magazine, January-June, 1900

Burlington, Ontario, Canada — www.apogeebooks.com
Cover and book design by Ron Miller

A HONEYMOON IN SPACE

Prologue

ABOUT EIGHT O'CLOCK ON THE MORNING of the 5th of November, 1900, those of the passengers and crew of the American liner St. Louis who happened, whether from causes of duty or of their own pleasure, to be on deck, had a very strange—in fact a quite unprecedented experience.

The big ship was ploughing her way through the long, smooth rollers at her average twenty-one knots towards the rising sun, when the officer in charge of the navigating bridge happened to turn his glasses straight ahead. He took them down from his eyes, rubbed the two object-glasses with the cuff of his coat, and looked again. The sun was shining through a haze which so far dimmed the solar disc that it was possible to look straight at it without inconvenience to the eyes.

The officer took another long squint, put his glasses down, rubbed his eyesanother, and murmured, "Well I'm damned!"

Just then the Fourth Officer came up on to the bridge to relieve his senior while he went down far a cup of coffee and a biscuit. The Second took him away to the other end of the bridge, out of hearing of the helmsman and the quartermaster standing by, and said almost in a whisper:

"Say, Norton, there's something ahead there that I can't make out. Just as the sun got clear above the horizon I saw a black spot go straight across it, right through the upper and lower limbs. I looked again, and it was plumb in the middle of the disc. Look," he went on, speaking louder in his growing excitement, "there it is again! I can see it without the glasses now. See?"

The Fourth did not reply at once. He had the glasses close to his eyes, and was moving them slowly about as though he were following some shifting object in the sky. Then he handed them back, and said:

"If I didn't believe the thing was impossible I should say that's an air-ship; but, for the present, I guess I'd rather wait till it gets a bit nearer, if it's coming. Still, there is something. Seems to be getting bigger pretty fast, too. Perhaps it would be as well to notify the old man. What do you think?"

"Guess we'd better," said the Second. "S'pose you go down. Don't say anything except to him. We don't want any more excitement among the people than we can help."

The Fourth nodded and went down the steps, and the Second began walking up and down the bridge, every now and then taking another squint ahead. Again and again the mysterious shape crossed the disc of the sun, always vertically as though, whatever it might be, it was steering a direct course from the sun to the ship, its apparent rising and falling being due really to the dipping of her bows into the swells.

"Well, Mr. Charteris, what's the trouble?" said the Skipper as he reached the bridge. "Nothing wrong, I hope? Have you sighted a derelict, or what? Ay, what in hell's that!"

His hands went up to his eyes and he stared for a few moments at the pale yellow oblate shape of the sun.

At this moment the St. Louis' head dipped again, and the Captain saw something like a black line swiftly drawn across the sun from bottom to top.

"That's what I wanted to call your attention to, sir," said the Second in a low tone. "I first noticed it crossing the sun as it rose through the mist. I thought it was a spot of dirt on my glasses, but it has crossed the sun several times since then, and for some minutes seemed to remain dead in the middle of it. Later on it got quite a lot larger, and whatever it is it's approaching us pretty rapidly. You see it's quite plain to the naked eye now."

By this time several of the crew and of the early loungers on deck had also caught sight of the strange thing which seemed to be hanging and swinging between the sky and the sea. People dived below for their glasses, knocked at their friends' state-room doors and told them to get up because something was flying towards the ship through the air; and in a very few minutes there were hundreds of passengers on deck in all varieties of early morning costume, and scores of glasses, held to anxious eyes, were being directed ahead.

The glasses, however, soon became unnecessary, for the passengers had scarcely got up on deck before the mysterious object to the eastward at length took definite shape, and as it did so mouths were opened as well as eyes, for the owners of the eyes and mouths beheld just then the strangest sight that travellers by sea or land had ever seen.

Within the distance of about a mile it swung round at right angles to the steamer's course with a rapidity which plainly showed that it was entirely obedient to the control of a guiding intelligence, and hundreds of eager eyes on board the liner saw, sweeping down from the grey-blue of the early morning sky, a vessel whose hull seemed to be constructed of some metal which shone with a pale, steely lustre.

It was pointed at both ends, the forward end being shaped something like a spur or ram. At the after end were two flickering, interlacing circles of a glittering greenish-yellow colour, apparently formed by two intersecting propellers driven at an enormous velocity. Behind these was a vertical fan of triangular shape. The craft appeared to be flat-bottomed, and for about a third of her length amidships the upper half of her hull was covered with a curving, dome-like roof of glass.

"She's an air-ship of some sort, there's no doubt about that," said the Captain, "so I guess the great problem has got solved at last. And yet it ain't a balloon, because it's coming against the wind, and it's nothing of the aeroplane sort neither, because it hasn't planes or kites or any fixings of that kind. Still it's made of something like metal and glass, and it must take a lot of keeping up. It's travelling at a pretty healthy speed too. Getting on for a hundred miles an hour, I should guess. Ah! he's going to speak us! Hope he's honest."

Everybody on board the St. Louis was up on deck by this time, and the excitement rose to fever-heat as the strange vessel swept down towards them from the middle sky, passed them like a flash of light, swung round the stern, and ranged up alongside to starboard some twenty feet from the bridge rail.

She was about a hundred and twenty feet long, with some twenty feet of depth and thirty of beam, and the Captain and many of his officers and passengers were very much relieved to find that, as far as could be seen, she carried no weapons of offence.

As she ranged up alongside, a sliding door opened in the glass-domed roof amidships, just opposite to the end of the St. Louis' bridge. A tall, fair-haired, clean-featured man, of about thirty, in grey flannels, tipped up his golf cap with his thumb, and said:

"Good morning, Captain! You remember me, I suppose? Had a fine passage, so far? I thought I should meet you somewhere about here."

The Captain of the St. Louis, in common with every one else on board, had already had his credulity stretched about as far as it would go, and he was beginning to wonder whether he was really awake; but when he heard the hail and recognised the speaker he stared at him in blank and, for the moment, speechless bewilderment. Then he got hold of his voice again and said, keeping as steady as he could:

"Good morning, my Lord! Guess I never expected to meet even you like this in the middle of the Atlantic! So the newspaper men were right for once in a way, and you have got an airship that will fly?"

"And a good deal more than that, Captain, if she wants to. I am just taking a trial trip across the Atlantic before I start on a run round the Solar System. Sounds like a lie, doesn't it? But it's coming off. Oh, good morning, Miss Rennick! Captain, may I come on board?"

"By all means, my Lord, only I'm afraid I daren't stop Uncle Sam's mails, even for you."

"There's no need for that, Captain, on a smooth sea like this," was the reply. "Just keep on as you are going and I'll come alongside."

He put his head inside the door and called something up a

speaking-tube which led to a glass walled chamber in the forward part of the roof, where a motionless figure stood before a little steering wheel.

The craft immediately began to edge nearer and nearer to the liner's rail, keeping speed so exactly with her that the threshold of the door touched the end of the bridge without a perceptible jar. Then the flannel-clad figure jumped on to the bridge and held out his hand to the Captain.

As they shook hands he said in a low tone, "I want a word or two in private with you, as soon as possible."

The commander saw a very serious meaning in his eyes. Besides, even if he had not made his appearance under such extraordinary circumstances, it was quite impossible that one of his social position and his wealth and influence could have made such a request without good reason for it, so he replied:

"Certainly, my Lord. Will you come down to my room?"

Hundreds of anxious, curious eyes looked upon the tall athletic figure and the regular-featured, bronzed, honest English face as Rollo Lenox Smeaton Aubrey, Earl of Redgrave, Baron Smeaton in the Peerage of England, and Viscount Aubrey in the Peerage of Ireland, followed the Captain to his room through the parting crowd of passengers. He nodded to one or two familiar faces in the crowd, for he was an old Atlantic ferryman, and had crossed five times with Captain Hawkins in the St. Louis.

Then he caught sight of a well and fondly remembered face which he had not seen for over two years. It was a face which possessed at once the fair Anglo-Saxon skin, the firm and yet delicate Anglo-Saxon features, and the wavy wealth of the old Saxon gold-brown hair; but a pair of big, soft, pansy eyes, fringed with long, curling, black lashes, looked out from under dark and perhaps Just a trifle heavy eye-brows. Moreover, there was that indescribable expression in the curve of her lips and the pose of her head; to say nothing of a lissome, vivacious grace in her whole carriage which proclaimed her a daughter of the younger branch of the Race that Rules.

Their eyes met for an instant, and Lord Redgrave as startled and even a trifle angered to see that she flushed up quickly, and that the momentary smile with which she greeted him died away as she turned her head aside. Still, he was a man accustomed to do what he wanted and what he wanted to do just then was to shake hands with Lilla Zaidie Rennick, and so he went straight towards her, raised his cap, and held out his hand saying, first with a glance into her eyes, and then with one upward at the Astronef:

"Good morning again, Miss Rennick! You see it is done."

"Good morning, Lord Redgrave!" she replied, he thought, a little awkwardly. "Yes, I see you have kept your promise. What a pity it is too late! But I hope you will be able to stop long enough to tell us all about it. This is Mrs. Van Stuyler, who has taken me under her protection on my journey to Europe."

His lordship returned the bow of a tall, somewhat hard-featured matron who looked dignified even in the somewhat nondescript costume which most of the ladies were wearing. But her eyes were kindly, and he said:

"Very pleased to meet, Mrs. Van Stuyler. I heard you were coming, and I was in hopes of catching you on the other side before you left. And now, if you will excuse me, I must go and have a chat with the Skipper. He raised his cap again and presently vanished from the curious eyes of the excited crowd, through the door of the Captain's apartment.

Captain Hawkins closed the door of his sitting-room as he entered, and said:

Now, my Lord, I'm not going to ask you any questions to begin with, because if I once began I should never stop; and besides, perhaps you'd like to have your own say right away."

"Perhaps that will be the shortest way," said his lordship. "The fact is, we've not only the remains of this Boer business on our hands, but we've had what is practically a declaration of war from France and Russia. Briefly it's this way. A few weeks ago, while the Allies thought they were fighting the Boxers, it came to the knowledge of my brother, the Foreign Secretary, that the Tsung-Li-Yamen had concluded a secret treaty with Russia which practically annulled all our rights over the Yang-tse Valley, and gave Russia the right to bring her Northern Railway right down through China.

"As you know, we've stood a lot too much in that part of the world already, but we couldn't stand this; so about ten days ago an ultimatum was sent declaring that the British government would consider any encroachment on the Yang-tse valley as an unfriendly act.

"Meanwhile France chipped in with a notification that she was going to occupy Morocco as a compensation for Fashoda, and added a few nasty things about Egypt and other places. Of course we couldn't stand that either, so there was another ultimatum, and the upshot of it all was that I got a wire late last night from my brother telling me that war would almost certainly be declared today, and asking me for the use of this craft of mine as a sort of dispatch- boat if she was ready. She is intended for something very much better than fighting purposes, so he couldn't ask me to use her as a war-ship; besides, I am under a solemn obligation to her inventor—her creator, in fact, for I've only built her—to blow her to pieces rather than allow her to be used as a fighting machine except, of course, in sheer personal self-defence.

"There is the telegram from my brother, so you can see there's no mistake, and just after it came a messenger asking me, if the machine was a success, to bring this with me across the Atlantic as fast as I could come. It is the duplicate of an offensive and defensive alliance between Great Britain and the United States, of which the details had been arranged just as this complication arose. Another is coming across by a fast cruiser, and, of course, the news will have got to Washington by cable by this time.

"By the time you get to the entrance of the Channel you will probably find it swarming with French cruisers and torpedo-destroyers, so if you'll be advised by me, you'll leave Queenstown out and get as far north as possible.

"Lord Redgrave," said the Captain, putting out his hand, "I'm responsible for a good bit right here, and I don't know how to thank you enough. I guess that treaty's been given away back to France by some of our Irish statesmen by now, and it'd be mighty unhealthy for the St. Louis to fall in with a French or Russian cruiser—"

"That's all right, Captain," said Lord Redgrave, taking his hand. "I should have warned any other British or American ship. At the same time, I must confess that my motives in warning you were not entirely unselfish. The fact is, there's some one on board the St. Louis whom I should decidedly object to see taken off to France as a prisoner of war."

"And may I ask who that is?" said Captain Hawkins.

"Why not?" replied his lordship. "It's the young lady I spoke to on deck just now, Miss Rennick. Her father was the inventor of that craft of mine. No one would believe his theories. He was refused patents both in England and America the ground of lack of practical utility. I met him about two years ago, that is to say rather more an a year before his death, when I was stopping at Banff up in the Canadian Rockies. We made a travellers' acquaintance, and he told me about this idea of his. I was very much interested, but I'm afraid I must confess that I might not have taken it practically if the Professor hadn't happened to possess an exceedingly beautiful daughter. However, of course I'm pretty glad now that I did do though the experiments cost nearly five thousand pounds and the craft herself close on a quarter of a million. Still, she is worth every penny of it, and I was bringing her over to offer to Miss Rennick as a wedding present, that is to say if she'd have it—and me."

Captain Hawkins looked up and said rather seriously:

"Then, my Lord, I presume you don't know—"

"Don't know what?"

"That Miss Rennick is crossing in the care of Mrs. Van Stuyler, to be married in London next month."

"The devil she is! And to whom, may I ask?" exclaimed his lordship, pulling himself up very straight.

"To the Marquis of Byfleet, son of the Duke of Duncaster. I wonder you didn't hear of it. The match was arranged last fall. From what people say she's not very desperately in love with him, but—well, I fancy it's like rather too many of these Anglo-American matches. A couple of million dollars on one side, a title on the other, and mighty little real love between them."

"But," said Redgrave between his teeth, "I didn't understand that Miss Rennick ever had a fortune; in fact I'm quite certain that if her father had been a rich man he'd have worked out his invention himself."

"Oh, the dollars aren't his. In fact they won't be hers till she marries," replied the Captain. "They belong to her uncle, old Russell Rennick. He got in on the ground floor of the New York and Chicago ice trusts, and made millions. He's going to spend some of them on making his niece a Marchioness. That's about all there is to it."

"Oh, indeed!" said Redgrave, still between his teeth. "Well, considering that Byfleet is about as big a wastrel as ever disgraced the English aristocracy, I don't think either Miss Rennick or her uncle will make a very good bargain. However, of course that's no affair of mine now. I remember that this Russell Rennick refused to finance his brother when he really wanted the money. He made a particularly bad bargain, too, then, though he didn't know it; for a dozen crafts like that, properly armed, would imply smash up the navies of the world, and make sea-power a private trust. After all, I'm not particularly sorry, because then it wouldn't have belonged to me. Well now, Captain, I'm going to ask you to give me a bit of breakfast when it's ready, then I must be off. I want to be in Washington to-night."

"To-night! What, twenty-one hundred miles!"

"Why not?" said Redgrave; "I can do about a hundred and fifty an hour through the atmosphere, and then, you see, if that isn't fast enough I can rise outside the earth's attraction, let it spin round, and then come down where I want to."

"Great Scott!" remarked Captain Hawkins inadequately, but with emphasis. "Well, my Lord, I guess we'll go down to breakfast."

But breakfast was not quite ready, and so Lord Redgrave rejoined Miss Rennick and her chaperon on deck. All eyes and a good many glasses were still turned on the Astronef, which had now moved a few feet away from the liner's side, and was running along, exactly keeping pace with her.

"It's so wonderful, that even seeing doesn't seem believing," said the girl, when they had renewed their acquaintance of two years before.

"Well," he replied, "it would be very easy to convince you. She shall come alongside again, and if you and Mrs. Van Stuyler will honour her by your presence for half an hour while breakfast is getting ready, I think I shall be able to convince you that she is not the airy fabric of a vision, but simply the realisation in metal and glass and other things of visions which your father saw some years ago."

There was no resisting an invitation put in such a way. Besides, the prospect of becoming the wonder and envy of every other woman on board was altogether too dazzling for words.

Mrs. Van Stuyler looked a little aghast at the idea at first, but she too had something of the same feeling as Zaidie, and besides, there could hardly be any impropriety in accepting the invitation of one of the wealthiest and most distinguished noblemen in the British Peerage. So, after a little demur and a slight manifestation of nervousness, she consented.

Redgrave signalled to the man at the steering wheel. The *Astronef* slackened pace a little, dropped a yard or so, and slid up quite close to the bridge-rail again. Lord Redgrave got in first and ran a light gangway down on to the bridge. Zaidie and Mrs. Van Stuyler were carefully handed up. The next moment the gangway was drawn up again, the sliding glass doors clashed to, the *Astronef* leapt a couple of thousand feet into the air, swept round to the westward in a magnificent curve, and vanished into the gloom of the upper mists.

Chapter 1

THE SITUATION WAS ONE which was absolutely without parallel in all the history of courtship from the days of Mother Eve to those of Miss Lilla Zaidie Rennick. The nearest approach to it would have been the old-fashioned Tartar custom which made it lawful for a man to steal his best girl, if he could get her first, fling her across his horse's crupper and ride away with her to his tent.

But to the shocked senses of Mrs. Van Stuyler the present adventure appeared a great deal more terrible than that. Both Zaidie and herself had sprung to their feet as soon as the upward rush of the *Astronef* had slackened and they were released from their seats. They looked down through the glass walls of what may be called the hurricane deck-chamber of the *Astronef*, and saw below them a snowy sea of clouds just crimsoned by the rising sun.

In this cloud-sea, which spread like a wide-meshed veil between them and the earth, there were great irregular rifts which looked as big as continents on a map. These had a blue-grey background, or it might be more correct to say under-ground, and in the midst of one of these they saw a little black speck which after a moment or two took the shape of a little toy ship, and presently they recognised it as the eleven-thousand-ton liner which a few moments ago had been their ocean home.

Mrs. Van Stuyler was shaking in every muscle, afflicted by a sort of St. Vitus' dance induced by physical fear and outraged propriety. Quite apart from these, however, she experienced a third sensation which made for a nameless inquietude. She was a woman of the world, well versed in most of its ways, and she fully recognised that that single bound from the bridge-rail of the St. Louis to the other side of the clouds had already carried her and her charge beyond the pale of human law.

The same thought, mingled with other feelings, half of wonder and half of re-awakened tenderness, was just then uppermost in Miss Zaidie's mind. It was quite obvious that the man who could create and control such a marvellous vehicle as this could, morally as well as physically, lift himself beyond the reach of the conventions which civilised society had instituted for its own protection and government.

He could do with them exactly as he pleased. They were utterly at his mercy. He might carry them away to some unexplored spot on one of the continents, or to some unknown island in the midst of the wide Pacific. He might even transport them into the midst of the awful solitudes which surround the Poles. He could give them the choice between doing as he wished, submitting unconditionally to his will, or committing suicide by starvation.

They had not even the option of jumping out, for they did not know how to open the sliding doors; and even if they had done, what feminine nerves could have faced a leap into that awful gulf which lay below them, a two-thousand-foot dive through the clouds into the waters of the wintry Atlantic?

They looked at each other in speechless, dazed amazement. Far away below them on the other side of the clouds the St. Louis was steaming eastward, and with her were going the last hopes of the coronet which was to be the matrimonial equivalent of Miss Zaidie's beauty and Russell Rennick's millions.

They were no longer of the world. Its laws could no longer protect them. Anything might happen, and that anything depended absolutely on the will of the lord and master of the extraordinary vessel which, for the present, was their only world.

"My dearest Zaidie!" Mrs. Van Stuyler gasped, when she at length recovered the power of articulate speech, "what an entirely too awful thing this is! Why, it's abduction and nothing less. Indeed it's worse, for he's taken us clean off the earth, and there's no more chance of rescue than if he took us to one of those planets he said he could go to. If I didn't feel a great responsibility for you, dear, I believe I should faint."

By this time Miss Zaidie had recovered a good deal of her usual composure. The excitement of the upward rush, and what was left of the momentary physical fear, had flushed her cheeks and lighted her eyes. Even Mrs. Van Stuyler thought her looking, if possible, more beautiful than she had done under the most favourable of terrestrial circumstances. There was a something else too, which she didn't altogether like to see, a sort of resignation to her fate which, in a young lady situated as she was then, Mrs. Van Stuyler considered to be distinctly improper.

"It is rather startling, isn't it?" she said, with hardly a trace of emotion in her voice; "but I have no doubt that everything will be all right in the end."

"Everything all right, my dear Zaidie! What on Earth, or I might say under heaven, do you mean?"

"I mean," replied Zaidie even more composedly than before, and also with a little tightening of her lips, "that Lord Redgrave is the owner of this vessel, and that therefore it is quite impossible that anything out of the way could happen to us—I mean anything more out of the way than this wonderful jump from the sea to the sky has been, unless, of course, Lord Redgrave is going to take us for a voyage among the stars."

"Zaidie Rennick!" said Mrs. Van Stuyler, bridling up into her most frigid dignity, "I am more than surprised to hear you talk in such a strain. Perfectly safe, indeed! Has it not struck you that we are absolutely at this man's—this Lord Redgrave's, mercy, that he can take us where he likes, and treat us just as he pleases?"

"My dear Mrs. Van," replied Zaidie, dropping back into her familiar form of address, but speaking even more frigidly than her chaperon had done, "you seem to forget that, however extraordinary our situation may be just now, we are in the care of an English gentleman. Lord Redgrave was a friend of my father's, the only man who believed in his ideals, the only man who realised them, the only man—"

"That you were ever in love with, eh?" said Mrs. Van Stuyler with a snap in her voice. "Is that so? Ah, I begin to see something now."

"And I think, if you possess your soul in patience, you will see something more before long," snapped Miss Zaidie in reply. Then she stopped abruptly and the flush on her cheek deepened, for at that moment Lord Redgrave came up the companion way from the lower deck carrying a big silver tray with a coffee pot, three cups and saucers, a rack of toast, and a couple of plates of bread and butter and cake.

Just then a sort of social miracle happened. The fact was that Mrs. Van Stuyler had never before had her early coffee brought to her by a peer of the British Realm. She thought it a little humiliating afterwards, but for the moment all sorts of conventional barriers seemed to melt away. After all she was a woman, and some years ago she had been a young one. Lord Redgrave was an almost perfect specimen of English manhood in its early prime. He was one of the richest peers in England, and he was bringing her her coffee. As she said afterwards, she wilted, and she couldn't help it.

"I'm afraid I have kept you waiting a long time for your coffee, ladies," said Redgrave, as he balanced the tray on one hand and drew a wicker table towards them with the other. "You see there are only two of us on board this craft, and as my engineer is navigating the ship, I have to attend to the domestic arrangements."

Mrs. Van Stuyler looked at him in the silence of mental paralysis. Miss Zaidie frowned, smiled, and then began to laugh.

"Well, of all the cold-blooded English ways of putting things—" she began.

"I beg your pardon?" said Lord Redgrave as he put the tray down on the table.

"What Miss Rennick means, Lord Redgrave," interrupted Mrs. Van Stuyler, struggling out of her paralytic condition, "and what I, too, should like to say, is that under the circumstances—"

"You think that I am not as penitent as I ought to be. Is that so?" said Redgrave, with a glance and a smile mostly directed towards Miss Zaidie.

"Well, to tell you the truth," he went on, "I am not a bit penitent. On the contrary, I am very glad to have been able to assist the Fates as far as I have done."

"Assist the Fates!" gasped Mrs. Van Stuyler, helping herself shakingly to sugar, while Miss Zaidie folded a gossamer slice of bread and butter and began to eat it; "I think, Lord Redgrave, that if you knew all the circumstances, you would say that you were working against them."

"My dear Mrs. Van Stuyler," he replied, as he filled his own coffee cup, "I quite agree with you as to certain fates, but the Fates which I mean are the ones which, with good or bad reason, I think are working on my side. Besides, I do know all the circumstances, or at least the most important of them. That knowledge is, in fact, my principal excuse for bringing you so unceremoniously above the clouds."

As he said this he took a sideway glance at Miss Zaidie. She dropped her eyelids and went on eating her bread and butter; but there was a little deepening of the flush on her cheeks which was to him as the first flush of sunrise to a benighted wanderer.

There was a rather awkward silence after this. Miss Zaidie stirred the coffee in her cup with a dainty Queen Anne spoon, and seemed to concentrate the whole of her attention upon the operation. Then Mrs. Van Stuyler took a sip out of her cup and said:

"But really, Lord Redgrave, I feel that I must ask you whether you think that what you have done during the last few minutes (which already, I assure you, seem hours to me) is—well, quite in accordance with the—what shall I say—ah, the rules that we have been accustomed to live under?"

Lord Redgrave looked at Miss Zaidie again. She didn't even raise her eyelids, only a very slight tremor of her hand as she raised her cup to her lips told that she was even listening. He took courage from this sign, and replied:

"My dear Mrs. Van Stuyler, the only answer that I can make to that just now is to remind you that, by the sanction of ages, everything is supposed to be fair under two sets of circumstances, and, whatever is happening on the earth down yonder, we, I think, are not at war."

The next moment Miss Zaidie's eyelids lifted a little. There was a tremor about her lips almost too faint to be perceptible, and the slightest possible tinge of colour crept upwards towards her eyes. She put her cup down and got up, walked towards the glass walls of the deck-chamber, and looked out over the cloud-scape.

The shortness of her steamer skirt made it possible for Lord Redgrave and Mrs. Van Stuyler to see that the sole of her right boot was swinging up and down on the heel ever so slightly. They came simultaneously to the conclusion that if she had been alone she would have stamped, and stamped pretty hard. Possibly also she would have said things to herself and the surrounding silence. This seemed probable from the almost equally imperceptible motion of her shapely shoulders.

Mrs. Van Stuyler recognised in a moment that her charge was getting angry. She knew by experience that Miss Zaidie possessed a very proper spirit of her own, and that it was just as well not to push matters too far. She further recognised that the circumstances were extraordinary, not to say equivocal, and that she herself occupied a distinctly peculiar position.

She had accepted the charge of Miss Zaidie from her Uncle Russell for a consideration counted partly by social advantages and partly by dollars. In the most perfect innocence she had permitted not only her charge but herself to be abducted—for, after all, that was what it came to—from the deck of an American liner, and carried, not only beyond the clouds, but also beyond the reach of human law, both criminal and conventional.

Inwardly she was simply fuming with rage. As she said afterwards, she felt just like a bottled volcano which would like to go off and daren't.

About two minutes of somewhat surcharged silence passed. Mrs. Van Stuyler sipped her coffee in ostentatiously small sips. Lord Redgrave took his in slower and longer ones, and helped himself to bread and butter. Miss Zaidie appeared perfectly contented with her contemplation of the clouds.

Chapter 2

AT LENGTH MRS. VAN STUYLER, being a woman of large experience and some social deftness, recognised that a change of subject was the easiest way of retreat out of a rather difficult situation. So she put her cup down, leant back in her chair, and, looking straight into Lord Redgrave's eyes, she said with purely feminine irrelevance:

"I suppose you know, Lord Redgrave, that, when we left, the machine which we call in America Manhood Suffrage—which, of course, simply means the selection of a government by counting noses which may or may not have brains above them—was what some of our orators would call in full blast. If you are going to New York after Washington, as you said on the boat, we might find it a rather inconvenient time to arrive. The whole place will be chaos, you know; because when the citizen of the United States begins electioneering, New York is not a very nice place to stop in except for people who want excitement, and so if you will excuse me putting the question so directly, I should like to know what you just do mean to do—"

Lord Redgrave saw that she was going to add" with us, "but before he had time to say anything, Miss Zaidie turned round, walked deliberately towards her chair, sat down, poured herself out a fresh cup of coffee, added the milk and sugar with deliberation, and then after a preliminary sip said, with her cup poised halfway between her dainty lips and the table:

"Mrs. Van, I've got an idea. I suppose it's inherited, for dear old Pop had plenty. Anyhow we may as well get back to common-sense subjects. Now look here," she went on, switching an absolutely convincing glance straight into her host's eyes, "my father may have been a dreamer, but still he was a Sound Money man. He believed in honest dealings. He didn't believe in borrowing a hundred dollars gold and paying back in fifty dollars silver. What's your opinion, Lord Redgrave; you don't do that sort of thing in England, do you? Uncle Russell is a Sound Money man too. He's got too much gold locked up to want silver for it."

"My dear Zaidie," said Mrs. Van Stuyler, "what have democratic and republican politics and bimetallism got to do with—"

"With a trip in this wonderful vessel which Pop told me years ago could go up to the stars if it ever was made? Why just this, Lord Redgrave is an Englishman and too rich to believe in anything but sound money, so is Uncle Russell, and there you have it, or should have."

"I think I see what you mean, Miss Rennick," said their host, leaning back in his chair and folding his hands behind his head, as steamboat travellers are wont to do when seas are smooth and skies are blue. "The *Astronef* might come down like a vision from the clouds and preach the Gospel of Gold in electric rays of silver through the commonplace medium of the Morse Code. How's that for poetry and practice?"

"I quite agree with his lordship as regards the practice," said Mrs. Van Stuyler, talking somewhat rudely across him to Zaidie. "It would be an excellent use to put this wonderful invention to. And then, I am sure his lordship would land us in Central Park, so that we could go to your Uncle's house right away."

"No, no, I'm afraid I must ask you to excuse me there, Mrs. Van Stuyler," said Redgrave, with a change of tone which Miss Zaidie appreciated with a swiftly veiled glance. "You see, I have placed myself beyond the law. I have, as you have been good enough to intimate, abducted—to put it brutally—two ladies from the deck of an Atlantic liner. Further, in doing so I have selfishly spoiled the prospects of one of the ladies. But, seriously, I really must go to Washington first—"

"I think, Lord Redgrave," interrupted Mrs. Van Stuyler, ignoring the last unfinished sentence and assuming her best Knickerbocker dignity, "if you will forgive me saying so, that that is scarcely a subject for discussion here."

"And if that's so," interrupted Miss Zaidie, "the less we say about it the better. What I wanted to say was this. We all want the Republicans in, at least all of us that have much to lose. Now, if Lord Redgrave was to use this wonderful air-ship of his on the right side—why there wouldn't be any standing against it.

"I must say that until just now I had hardly contemplated turning the *Astronef* into an electioneering machine. Still, I admit that she might be made use of in a good cause, only I hope—"

"That we shan't want you to paste her over with election bills, eh?—or start handbill-snowstorms from the deck—or kidnap Croker and Bryan just as you did us, for instance?"

"If I could, I'm quite sure that I shouldn't have as pleasant guests as I have now on board the *Astronef*. What do you think, Mrs. Van Stuyler?"

"My dear Lord Redgrave," she replied, "that would be quite impossible. The idea of being shut up in a ship like this which can soar not only from earth, but beyond the clouds, with people who would find out your best secrets and then perhaps shoot you so as to be the only possessors of them—well, that would he foolishness indeed."

"Why, certainly it would," said Zaidie; "the only use you could have for people like that would be to take them up above the clouds and drop them out. But suppose we—I mean Lord Redgrave—took the *Astronef* down over New York and signalled messages from the sky at night with a searchlight—"

"Good," said their host, getting up from his deck-chair and stretching himself up straight, looking the while at Miss Zaidie's averted profile. "That's gorgeously good! We might even turn the election. I'm for sound money all the time, if I may be permitted to speak American."

"English is quite good enough for us, Lord Redgrave, "said Miss Zaidie a little stiffly. "We may have improved on the old language a bit, still we understand it, and—well, we can forgive its shortcomings. But that isn't quite to the point."

"It seems to me," said Mrs. Van Stuyler, "that we are getting nearly as far from the original subject as we are from the St. Louis. May I ask, Zaidie, what you really propose to do?"

"Do is not for us to say," said Miss Zaidie, looking straight up to the glass roof of the deck-chamber. "You see, Mrs. Van, we're not free agents. We are not even first-class passengers who have paid their fares on a contract ticket which is supposed to get them there."

"If you'll pardon me saying so," said Lord Redgrave, stopping his walk up and down the deck, "that is not quite the case. To put it in the most brutally material form, it is quite true that I have kidnapped you two ladies and taken you beyond the reach of earthly law. But there is another law, one which would bind a gentleman even if he were beyond the limits of the Solar System, and so if you wish to be landed either in Washington or New York it shall be done. You shall be put down within a carriage drive of your own residence, or of Mr. Russell Rennick's. I will myself see you to his door, and there we may say goodbye, and I will take my trip through the Solar System alone."

There was another pause after this, a pause pregnant with the fate of two lives. They looked at each other—Mrs. Van Stuyler at Zaidie, Zaidie at Lord Redgrave, and he at Mrs Van Stuyler again. It was a kind of three-cornered duel of eyes, and the eyes said a good deal more than common human speech could have done.

Then Lord Redgrave, in answer to the last glance from Zaidie's eyes, said slowly and deliberately:

"I don't want to take any undue advantage, but I think I am justified in making one condition. Of course I can take you beyond the limits of the world that we know, and to other worlds that we know little or nothing of. At least I could do so if I were not bound by law as strong as gravitation itself; but now, as I said before, I just ask whether or not my guests or, if you think it suits the circumstances better, my prisoners, shall be released unconditionally wherever they choose to be landed."

He paused for a moment and then, looking straight into Zaidie's eyes, he added:

"The one condition I make is that the vote shall be unanimous."

"Under the circumstances, Lord Redgrave," said Mrs. Van Stuyler, rising from her seat and walking towards him with all the dignity that would have been hers in her own drawing-room, "there can only be one answer to that. Your guests or your prisoners, as you choose to call them, must be released unconditionally."

Lord Redgrave heard these words as a man might hear words in a dream. Zaidie had risen too. They were looking into each other's eyes, and many unspoken words were passing between them. There was a little silence, and then, to Mrs. Van Stuyler's unutterable horror, Zaidie said, with just the suspicion of a gasp in her voice:

"There's one dissentient. We are prisoners, and I guess I'd better surrender at discretion."

The next moment her captor's arm was round her waist, and Mrs. Van Stuyler, with her twitching fingers linked behind her back, and her nose at an angle of sixty degrees, was staring away through the blue immensity, dumbly wondering what on earth or under heaven was going to happen next.

CHAPTER 3

AFTER A COUPLE OF MINUTES of silence which could be felt, Mrs. Van Stuyler turned round and said angrily:

"Zaidie, you will excuse me, perhaps, if I say that your conduct is not—I mean has not been what I should have expected—what I did, indeed, expect from your uncle's niece when I undertook to take you to Europe. I must say—"

"If I were you, Mrs. Van, I don't think I'd say much more about that, because, you see, it's fixed and done. Of course, Lord Redgrave's only an earl, and the other is a marquis, but, you see, he's a man, and I don't quite think the other one is—and that's about all there is to it."

Their host had just left the deck-saloon, taking the early coffee apparatus with him, and Miss Zaidie, in the first flush of her pride and re-found happiness, was taking a promenade of about twelve strides each way, while Mrs. Van Stuyler, after partially relieving her feelings as above, had seated herself stiffly in her wicker-chair, and was following her with eyes which were critical and, if they had been twenty years younger, might also have been envious.

"Well, at least I suppose I must congratulate you on your ability to accommodate yourself to most extraordinary circumstances. I must say that as far as that goes I quite envy you. I feel as though I ought to choke or take poison, or something of that sort."

"Sakes, Mrs. Van, please don't talk like that!" said Zaidie, stopping in her walk just in front of her chaperon's chair. "Can't you see that there's nothing extraordinary about the circumstances except this wonderful ship? I have told you how Pop and I met Lord

Redgrave in our tour through the Canadian Rockies two or three years ago. No, it's two years and nine months next June; and how he took an interest in Pop's theories and ideas about this same ship that we are on now—"

"Oh yes," said Mrs. Van Stuyler rather acidly, "and not only in the abstract ideas, but apparently in a certain concrete reality."

"Mrs. Van," laughed Zaidie, with a cunning twist on her heel, "I know you don't mean to be rude, but—well, now did any one ever call you a concrete reality? Of course it's correct just as a scientific definition, perhaps—still, anyhow, I guess it's not much good going on about that. The facts are just this way. I consented to marry that Byfleet marquis just out of sheer spite and blank ignorance. Lord Redgrave never actually asked me to marry him when we were in the Rockies, but he did say when he went back to England that as soon as he had realised my father's ideal he would come over and try and realise one of his own. He was looking at me when he said it, and he looked a good deal more than he said. Then he went away, and poor Pop died. Of course I couldn't write and tell him, and I suppose he was too proud to write before he'd done what he undertook to do, and I, like most girl-fools in the same place would have done, thought that he'd given the whole thing up and just looked upon the trip as a sort of interlude in globe-trotting, and thought no more about Pop's ideas and inventions than he did about his daughter."

"Very natural, of course," said Mrs. Van Stuyler, somewhat mollified by the subdued passion which Zaidie had managed to put into her commonplace words; "and so as you thought he had forgotten you and was finding a wife in his own country, and a possible husband came over from that same country with a coronet—"

"That'll do, Mrs. Van, thank you," interrupted Miss Zaidie, bringing her daintily-shod foot down on the deck this time with an unmistakable stamp. "We'll consider that incident closed if you please. It was a miserable, mean, sordid business altogether; I am utterly, hopelessly ashamed of it and myself too. Just to think that I could ever—"

Mrs. Van Stuyler cut short her indignant flow of words by a sudden uplifting of her eyelids and a swift turn of her head towards the companion way. Zaidie stamped again, this time more softly, and walked away to have another look at the clouds.

"Why, what on earth is the matter?" she exclaimed, shrinking back from the glass wall. "There's nothing—we're not anywhere!"

"Pardon me, Miss Rennick, you are on board the *Astronef*," said Lord Redgrave, as he reached the top of the companion way, "and the *Astronef* is at present travelling at about a hundred and fifty miles an hour above the clouds towards Washington. That is why you don't see the clouds and sea as you did after we left the St. Louis. At a speed like this they simply make a sort of grey-green blur. We shall be in Washington this evening, I hope."

"To-night, sir—I beg your pardon, my Lord!" gasped Mrs. Van Stuyler. "A hundred and fifty miles an hour! Surely that's impossible."

"My dear Mrs. Van Stuyler," said Redgrave, with a side-look at Zaidie, "nowadays 'impossible' is hardly an English or even an American word. In fact, since I have had the honour of realising some of Professor Rennick's ideas it has been relegated to the domain of mathematics. Not even he could make two and two more or less than four, but—well, would you like to come into the conning-tower and see for yourselves? I can show you a few experiments that will, at any rate, help to pass the time between here and Washington."

"Lord Redgrave," said Mrs. Van Stuyler, dropping gracefully back into her wicker armchair, "if I may say so, I have seen quite enough impossibilities, and—er, well—other things since we left the deck of the St. Louis to keep me quite satisfied until, with your Lordship's permission, I set foot on solid ground again, and I should also like to remind you that we have left everything behind us on the St. Louis, everything except what we stand up in, and—and—"

"And therefore it will be a point of honour with me to see that you want for nothing while you are on board the *Astronef*, and that you shall be released from your durance—"

"Now don't say vile, Lenox— I mean—"

"It is perfectly plain what you mean, Zaidie," said Mrs. Van Stuyler, in a tone which seemed to send a chill through the deck-chamber. "Really, the American girl—"

"Just wants to tell the truth," laughed Zaidie, going towards Redgrave. "Lord Redgrave, if you like it better, says he wants to marry me, and, peer or peasant, I want to marry him, and that's all there is to it. You don't suppose I'd have—"

"My dear girl, there's no need to go into details," interrupted Mrs. Van Stuyler, inspired by fond memories of her own youth; "we will take that for granted, and as we are beyond the social region in which chaperons are supposed to be necessary, I think I will have a nap."

"And we'll go to the conning-tower, eh?"

"Breakfast will be ready in about half an hour," said Redgrave, as he took Zaidie by the arm and led her towards the forward end of the deck-chamber. "Meanwhile, au revoir! If you want anything, touch the button at your right hand, just as you would on board the St. Louis."

"I thank your lordship," said Mrs. Van Stuyler, half melting and half icy still. "I shall be quite content to wait until you come back. Really I feel quite sleepy."

"That's the effect of the elevation on the dear old lady's nerves," Redgrave whispered to Zaidie as he helped her up the narrow stairway which led to the glass domed conning-tower, in which in days to come she was destined to pass some of the most delightful and the most terrible moments of her life.

"Then why doesn't it affect me that way?" said Zaidie, as she took her place in the little chamber, steel-walled and glass-roofed, and half filled with instruments of which she, Vassar girl and all as she was, could only guess the use.

"Well, to begin with, you are younger, which is an absolutely unnecessary observation; and in the second place, perhaps you were thinking about something else."

"By which I suppose you mean your lordship's noble self."

This was said in such a tone and with such an indescribable

smile that there immediately ensued a gap in the conversation, and a silence which was a great deal more eloquent than any words could have made it.

When Miss Zaidie had got free again she put her hands up to her hair, and while she was patting it into something like shape again she said:

"But I thought you brought me here to show me some experiments, and not to—"

"Not to take advantage of the first real opportunity of tasting some of the dearest delights that mortal man ever stole from earth or sea? Do you remember that day when we were coming down from the big glacier—when your foot slipped and I just caught you and saved a sprained ankle?"

"Yes, you wretch, and went away next day and left something like a broken heart behind you! Why didn't you—Oh what idiots you men can be when you put your minds to it!"

"It wasn't quite that, Zaidie. You see, I'd promised your father the day before—of course I was only a younger son then—that I wouldn't say anything about realising my ideal until I had realised his, and so—"

"And so I might have gone to Europe with Uncle Russell's millions to buy that man Byfleet's coronet, and pay the price—"

"Don't, Zaidie, don't! That is quite too horrible to think of, and as for the coronet, well, I think I can give you one about as good as his, and one that doesn't want re-gilding. Good Lord, fancy you married to a thing like that! What could have made you think of it?"

"I didn't think," she said angrily; "I didn't think and I didn't feel. Of course I thought that I'd dropped right out of your life, and after that I didn't care. I was mad right through, and I'd made up my mind to do what others did—take a title and a big position, and have the outside as bright as I could get it, whatever the inside might be like. I'd made up my mind to be a society queen abroad, and a miserable woman at home— and, Lenox, thank God and you, that I wasn't!"

Then there was another interlude, and at the end of it Redgrave said:

"Wait till we've finished our honeymoon in space, and come

back to earth. You won't want any coronets then, although you'll have one, for all the lands of earth won't hold another woman like yourself—your own sweet self! Of course it doesn't now, but there, you know what I mean. You'll have been to other worlds, you'll have made the round trip of the Solar System, so to say, and—"

"And I think, dear, that is about promise of wonders enough, and of other things too—no, you're really quite too exacting. I thought you brought me here to show me some of the wonders that this marvellous ship of yours can work."

"Then just one more and I'll show you. Now you stand up there on that step so that you can see all round, and watch with all your eyes, because you are going to see something that no woman ever saw before."

Chapter 4

Above a tiny little writing-desk fixed to the wall of the conning-tower there was a square mahogany board with six white buttons in pairs. On one side of the board hung a telephone and on the other a speaking-tube. To the right hand opposite where Zaidie stood were two nickel—plated wheels and behind each of them a white disc, one marked off into 360 degrees, and the other into 100 with subdivisions of tens. Overhead hung an ordinary tell-tale compass, and compactly placed on other parts of the wall were barometers, thermometers, barographs, and, in fact, practically every instrument that the most exacting of aeronauts or space-explorers could have asked for.

"You see, Zaidie, this is what one might call the cerebral chamber of the *Astronef* and, granted that my engines worked all right, I could make her do anything I wanted without moving out of here, but as a rule, of course, Murgatroyd is in the engine-room. If he wasn't the most whole-souled Wesleyan that Yorkshire ever produced, I believe he'd become an idolater and worship the *Astronef*'s engines."

"And who is Murgatroyd, please?"

"In the first place he is what I might call an hereditary retainer of the House of Redgrave. His ancestors have served mine for the last seven hundred years. When my ancestors were burglar-barons, his were men-at-arms. When we went on the Crusades they went too; when we raised a regiment for the King against the Parliament they were naturally the first to enlist in it; and as we gradually settled down into peaceful respectability they did the same. Lastly, when we went into trade as ironmasters and engineers they went in too. This Murgatroyd, for instance, was master-foreman of my works at Smeaton, and he was the only man I dared trust with the secrets of the *Astronef*, and the only one I would trust myself on board her with, and that's why we're a crew of two. You see the command of a vessel like this is a fairly big business, and if it got into the wrong sort of hands—"

"Yes, I see," said Zaidie with a little nod. It would be just too awful to think about. Why you might keep the world in terror with it; but I know you wouldn't do that, because, for one thing, I wouldn't let you."

"Gently, gently, Ma'm'selle; permit me most humbly to remind you that you are still my prisoner, and that I am still Commander of the *Astronef*."

"Oh, very well then," said Zaidie, interrupting him with a pretty little gesture of impatience, "and now suppose you let me see what the *Astronef*'s commander can do with her."

"Certainly," replied Redgrave, "and with the greatest pleasure—but, by the way, that reminds me you haven't paid your footing yet."

When due payment had been given and taken, or perhaps it would be more correct to say taken and given, Redgrave put his finger on one of the buttons.

Immediately Zaidie heard the swish of the air past the smooth wall of the conning-tower grow fainter and fainter. Then there came a little check which nearly upset her balance, and presently the clouds beneath them began to take shape and great white continents of them with grey oceans in between went sweeping silently and swiftly away behind them.

Redgrave turned the wheel in front of the 100-degree disc a little to the left. The next instant the clouds rose up. For a moment Zaidie could see nothing but white mist on all sides. Then the atmosphere cleared again, and she saw far below her what looked like a vast expanse of ocean that had been suddenly frozen solid.

There were the long Atlantic rollers tipped with snowy foam. Here and there at wide intervals were little black dots, some of them with brown trails behind them, others with little patches of white which showed up distinctly against the dark grey-blue of the sea. Every moment they grew bigger. Then the white-crested waves began to move, and the big ocean steamers and full-rigged sailing ships looked less and less like toys. Just under them there was a very big one with four funnels pouring out dense volumes of black smoke. Redgrave took up a pair of glasses, looked at her for a moment and said:

"That's the Deutschland, the new Hamburg-American record-breaker. Suppose we go down and have a lark with her. I wonder if she's taking news of the war. We're in with Germany, and they may know something about it."

"That would be just too lovely!" said Zaidie. "Let's go and show them how we can break records. I suppose they've seen us by this time and are just wondering with all their wits what we are. I guess they'll feel pretty tired about poor Count Zeppelin's balloon when they see us."

Redgrave noted the "we" and the "us" with much secret satisfaction.

"All right," he said, "we'll go and give them a bit of a startler."

In front of the conning-tower there was a steel flagstaff about tell feet high, with halliards rove through a sheer in the top. He took a little roll of bunting out of a locker under the desk, opened a glass slide, brought in the halliards and bent the flag on.

Meanwhile the long shape of the great liner was getting bigger and bigger. Her decks were black with people staring up at this strange apparition which was dropping upon them from the clouds. Another minute and the *Astronef* had dropped to within five hundred feet of the water, and about half a mile astern of the Deutschland. Redgrave turned the wheel back two or three inches and touched a second button.

The *Astronef* stopped her descent instantly, and then she shot forward. The new greyhound was making her twenty-two and a half knots, hurling a broad white torrent of foam away from under her counters. But in half a minute the *Astronef* was alongside her.

Redgrave ran the roll of bunting up to the top of the flagstaff, pulled one of the halliards, and the White Ensign of England floated out. Almost at the same moment the German flag went up to the staff at the stern of the Deutschland, and they heard a roar of cheers, mingled with cries of wonder, come up from her swarming decks.

Each flag was dipped thrice in due course. Redgrave took off his cap and bowed to the Captain on the bridge. Zaidie nodded and fluttered her handkerchief in reply to hundreds of others that were waving on the decks. Mrs. Van Stuyler woke up in wonder and waved hers instinctively, half longing to change crafts. In fact, if it hadn't been for her absolute devotion to the proprieties she would have obeyed her first impulse and asked Lord Redgrave to put her on board the steamer.

While the officers and crew and passengers of the Deutschland were staring wide-eyed and open-mouthed at the graceful glittering shape of the *Astronef*, Redgrave touched the first button in the second row once, moved the 100-degree wheel on a few degrees, and then gave the other a quarter turn. Then he closed the window slide, and the next moment Zaidie saw the great liner sink down beneath them in a curious twisting sort of way. She seemed to stop still and then spin round on her centre, getting smaller and smaller every moment.

"What's the matter, Lenox?" she said, with a little gasp. "What's the Deutschland doing? She seems to be spinning round on her own axis like a top."

"That's only the point of view, dear. She's just plugging along straight on her way to New York, and we've been making rings round her and going up all the time. But of course you don't notice the motion here any more than you would if you were in a balloon."

"But I thought you were going to speak to them. Surely you don't mean to say that you intended that just as a little bit of showing off?"

"That's about what it comes to, I suppose, but you must not think it was altogether vanity. You see the German Government has bought Count Zeppelin's air-ship or steerable balloon, as it ought to be called, always supposing that they can steer it in a wind, and of course their idea is to make a fighting machine of it. Now Germany is engaged to stand by us in this trouble that's coming, and by way of cementing the alliance I thought it was just as well to let the wily Teuton know that there's something flying the British flag which could make very small mincemeat of their gas-bags."

"And what about Old Glory?" said Miss Zaidie. "The *Astronef* was built with English money and English skill, but—"

"She is the creature of American genius. Of course she is. In fact she is the first concrete symbol of the Anglo-American Alliance, and when the daughter of her creator has gone into partnership with the man who made her we'll have two flagstaffs, and the Jack and Old Glory will float side by side."

"And meanwhile where are we going?" asked Zaidie, after a moment's interval. "Ah, there we are through the clouds again. What makes us rise? Is that the force that Pop told me he discovered?"

"I'll answer the last question first," said Redgrave. "That was the greatest of your father's discoveries. He got at the secret of gravitation, and was able to analyse it into two separate forces just as Volta did with electricity—positive and negative, or, to put it better, attractive and repulsive.

"Three out of the five sets of engines in the *Astronef* develop the R. Force, as I call it for short. This wheel with the hundred degrees marked behind it regulates the development. The further I turn it this way to the right, the more the R. Force overcomes the attractive force of the earth or any other planet that we may visit. Turn it back, and gravitation asserts itself. If I put this arrow-head on the wheel opposite zero the weight of the *Astronef* is about a hundred and fifty tons, and of course she would go down like a stone, and a very big one at that. At ten she weighs nothing; that is to say the R Force exactly counteracts gravitation. At eleven she begins to rise. At a hundred she would be hurled away from the earth like a shell from a twelve-inch gun, or even faster. Now, watch."

He took up the speaking-tube. "Is she all tight everywhere, Andrew?"

"Yes, my Lord," came gurgling through the tube.

Then Redgrave slowly turned the wheel till the indicator pointed to twenty-five. Zaidie, all eyes and wonder, saw a vast sea of glittering white spread out beneath them, an ocean of snow with grey-blue patches here and there. It sank away from under them till the patches became spots and the sunlit clouds a vast, luminous blur. The air about them grew marvellously clear and limpid. The sun blazed down on them with a tenfold intensity of light, but Zaidie was astonished to find that very little heat penetrated the glass walls and roof of the conning-tower.

"What an awful height!" she exclaimed, looking round at him with something like fear in her eyes. "How high are we, Lenox?"

"You'll find afterwards that the *Astronef* doesn't take any account of high or low or up or down," he replied, looking at the dial of an aneroid barometer by the side of him. "Roughly speaking, we're rather over 60,000 feet—say ten miles—from the surface of the Atlantic. That's why I asked Andrew whether everything was tight. You see we couldn't breathe the air there is outside there—too thin and cold—and so the *Astronef* makes her own atmosphere as we go along. But I won't spoil what you're going to see by any more of this. So if you please, we'll go down now and get along to Washington. Anyhow, I hope I've convinced you so far that I've kept my promise."

"Yes, dear, you have, and splendidly! I've only one regret. If he was only here now, what a happy man he'd be! Still, I daresay he knows all about it and is just as happy. In fact he must be. I feel certain he must. The very soul of his intellect was in the dream of this ship, and now that it's a reality he must he here still. Isn't it part of himself? Isn't it his mind that's working in these wonderful engines of yours, and isn't it his strength that lifts us up from the earth and takes us down again just as you please to turn that wheel?"

"There's little doubt about that, Zaidie," said Redgrave quietly, but earnestly. "You know we North-country folk all have our traditions and our ghosts; and what more likely than that the spirit of a dead man or a man gone to other worlds should watch over the realisation of his greatest work on earth? Why shouldn't we believe that, we who are going away from this world to other ones?"

"Why not?" interrupted Zaidie, "why, of course we will. And now suppose we come down in more ways than one and go and give poor Mrs. Van Stuyler something to eat and drink. The dear old girl must be frightened half out of her wits by this time."

"Very well," replied Redgrave; "but we'll come down literally first, so that we can get the propellers to work."

He turned the wheel back till the indicator pointed to five. The cloud-sea came up with a rush. They passed through it, and stopped about a thousand feet above the sea. Redgrave touched the first button twice, and then the next one twice. The air began to hiss past the walls of the conning-tower. The crest-crowned waves of the Atlantic seemed to sweep in a hurrying torrent behind them, and then Redgrave, having made sure that Murgatroyd was at the after-wheel, gave him the course for Washington, and then went down to induct his bride-elect into the art and mystery of cooking by electricity as it was done in the kitchen of the *Astronef.*

Chapter 5

As this narrative is the story of the personal adventures of Lord Redgrave and his bride, and not an account of events at which all the world has already wondered, there is no necessity to describe in any detail the extraordinary sequence of circumstances which began when the *Astronef* dropped without warning from the clouds in front of the White House at Washington, and his lordship, after paying his respects to the President, proceeded to the British Embassy and placed the copy of the Anglo-American agreement in Lord Pauncefote's hands.

Mrs. Van Stuyler's spirits had risen as the *Astronef* descended towards the lights of Washington, and when the President and Lord Pauncefote paid a visit to the wonderful craft, the joint product of American genius and English capital and constructive skill, she immediately assumed, at Redgrave's request, the position of lady of the house pro tem, and described the "change of plans," as she called it, which led to their transfer from the St. Louis to the *Astronef* with an imaginative fluency which would have done credit to the most enterprising of American interviewers.

"You see, my dear," she said to Zaidie afterwards, "as everything turned out so very happily, and as Lord Redgrave behaved in such a splendid way, I thought it was my duty to make everything appear as pleasant to the President and Lord Pauncefote as I could."

"It was real good of you, Mrs. Van," said Zaidie. "If I hadn't been paralysed with admiration I believe I should have laughed.

Now if you'll just come with us on our trip, and write a book about it afterwards just as you told—I mean as you described what happened between the St. Louis and Washington, to the President and Lord Pauncefote, you'd make a million dollars out of it. Say now, won't you come?"

"My dear Zaidie," Mrs. Van Stuyler replied, "you know that I am very fond of you. If I'd only had a daughter I should have wanted her to be just like you, and I should have wanted her to marry a man just like Lord Redgrave. But there's a limit to everything. You say that you are going to the moon and the stars, and to see what the other planets are like. Well, that's your affair. I hope God will forgive you for your presumption, and let you come back safe, but I——No. Ten—twenty millions wouldn't pay me to tempt Providence like that."

The *Astronef* had landed in front of the White House, as everybody knows, on the eve of the Presidential election. After dinner in the deck-saloon, as the Space Navigator lay in the midst of a square of troops, outside which a huge crowd surged and struggled to get a look at the latest miracle of constructive science, the President and the British Ambassador said goodbye, and as soon as the gang-way ladder was drawn in the *Astronef*, moved by no visible agency, rose from the ground amidst a roar of cheers coming from a hundred thousand throats. She stopped at a height of about a thousand feet, and then her forward searchlight flashed out, swept the horizon, and vanished. Then it flashed out again intermittently in the longs and shorts of the Morse Code, and these, when translated, read:

"Vote for sound men and sound money!"

In five minutes the wires of the United States were alive with the terse, pregnant message, and under the ocean in the dark depths of the Atlantic ooze, vivid narratives of the coming of the miracle went flashing to a hundred newspaper offices in England and on the Continent. The New York correspondent of the London Daily Express added the following paragraph to his account of the strange occurrence:

"The secret of this amazing vessel, which has proved itself

capable of traversing the Atlantic in a day, and of soaring beyond the limits of the atmosphere at will, is possessed by one man only, and that man is an English nobleman. The air is full of rumours of universal war. One vessel such as this could scatter terror over a continent in a few days, demoralise armies and fleets, reduce Society to chaos, and establish a one-man despotism on the ruins of all the Governments of the world. The man who could build one ship like this could build fifty, and, if his country asked him to do it, no doubt he would. Those who, as we are almost forced to believe, are even now contemplating a serious attempt to dethrone England from her supreme place among the nations of Europe, will do well to take this latest potential factor in the warfare of the immediate future into their most serious consideration."

This paragraph was not perhaps as absolutely correct as a proposition in Euclid, but it stopped the war. The Deutschland came in the next day, and again the press was flooded, this time with personal narratives, and brilliantly imaginative descriptions of the vision which had descended from the clouds, made rings round the great liner going at her best speed, and then vanished in an instant beyond the range of field-glasses and telescopes.

Thus did the creature of Professor Rennick's inventive genius play its first part as the peacemaker of the world.

When the *Astronef*'s message had been duly given and recorded, her propellers began to revolve, and her head swung round to the north-east. So began, as all the world now knows, the most extraordinary electioneering trip that ever was known. First Baltimore, then Philadelphia, and then New York saw the flashes in the sky. There were illuminations, torchlight processions, and all the machinery of American electioneering going at full blast. But when people saw, far away up in the starlit night, those swiftly-changing beams glittering down, as it were, out of infinite Space, and when the telegraph operators caught on to the fact that they were signals, a sort of awe seemed to come over both Republicans and Democrats alike. Even Tammany's thoughts began to lift above the sordid level of boodle. It was almost like a message from another world. There was something supernatural about it, and when it was translated and rushed out in extra editions of the evening papers: "Vote for sound men and sound money" became the watchword of millions.

From New York to Boston, Boston to Albany, and then across country to Buffalo, Cleveland, Chicago, Omaha—then westward to St. Paul and Minneapolis, and northward to Portland and Seattle, southward to San Francisco and Monterey, then eastward again to Salt Lake City, and then, after a leap across the Rockies which frightened Mrs Van Stuyler almost to fainting point and made Zaidie gasp for breath, away southward to Santa Fe and New Orleans.

Then northward again up the Mississippi Valley to St. Louis, and thence eastward across the Alleghanies back to Washington—such was the famous night-voyage of the *Astronef*, and so by means of that long silver tongue of light did she spread the message of common-sense and commercial honesty throughout the length and breadth of the Great Republic. The world knows how America received and interpreted it the next day.

Meanwhile Mr. Russell Rennick had taken train to Washington, and the day after the election he willingly took back all that he had intended with regard to the Marquis of Byfleet, accepted Lord Redgrave in his stead, and bestowed his avuncular blessing at the wedding breakfast held in the deck-chamber of the *Astronef* poised in mid-air, five hundred feet above the dome of the Capitol, a week later. To this he added a cheque for a million dollars—payable to the Countess of Redgrave on her return from her wedding trip.

Breakfast over, the wedding party made an inspection of the wonderful vessel under the guidance of her Commander. After this, while they were drinking their coffee and liqueurs, and the men were smoking their cigars in the deck-chamber, a score of the most distinguished men and women in the United States experienced the novel sensation of sitting quietly in deck-chairs while they were being hurled at the rate of a hundred and fifty miles an hour through the atmosphere.

They ran up to Niagara, dropped to within a few feet of the surface of the Falls, passed over them, fell to the Rapids, and drifted down them within a couple of yards of the raging waters. Then in an instant they leapt up into the clouds, dropped again, and took a slanting course for Washington at a speed incredible, but to them quite imperceptible, save for the blurred rush of the half-visible earth behind them.

That night the *Astronef* rested again in front of the steps of the White House, and Lord and Lady Redgrave were the guests at a semi-official banquet given by the newly re-elected President. The speech of the evening was made by the President himself in proposing the health of the bride and bridegroom, and this is the way he ended:

"There is something more in the ceremony which we have been privileged to witness than the union of a man and a woman in the bonds of holy matrimony. Lord Redgrave, as you know, is the descendant of one of the noblest and most ancient families in the Motherland of New Nations. Lady Redgrave is the daughter of the oldest and, I hope I may be allowed to say without offence, the greatest of those nations. It is, perhaps, early days to talk about a formal federation of the Anglo-Saxon people, but I think I am only voicing the sentiments of every good American when I say that, if the rumours which have drifted over and under the Atlantic, rumours of a determined attempt on the part of certain European powers to assault and, if possible, destroy that magnificent fortress of individual liberty and collective equity which we call the British Empire should unhappily prove to be true, then it may be that the rest of the world will find that America does not speak English for nothing.

"But I must also remind you that a few yards from the doors of the White House there lies the greatest marvel, I had almost said the greatest miracle, that has ever been accomplished by human genius and human industry. That wonderful vessel in which some of us have been privileged to take the most marvellous journey in the history of mechanical locomotion was thought out by an American man of science, the man whose daughter sits on my right hand tonight. In her concrete material form this vessel, destined to navigate the shoreless Ocean of Space, is English. But she is also the result of the belief and the faith of an Englishman in an American ideal.... So when she leaves this earth, as she will do in an hour or so, to enter the confines of other worlds than this—and, it may be, to make the acquaintance of peoples other than those who inhabit the earth—she will have done infinitely more than she has already done, incredible as that seems. She will not only have convinced this world that the greatest triumph of human genius is of Anglo-Saxon origin, but she will carry to other worlds than this the truth which this world will have learnt before the nineteenth century ends.

"England in the person of Lord Redgrave, and America in the person of his Countess, leave this world to-night to tell the other worlds of our system, if haply they may find some intelligible means of communication, what this world, good and bad, is like. And it is within the bounds of possibility that in doing so they may inaugurate a wider fellowship of created beings than the limits of this world permit; a fellowship, a friendship, and, as the *Astronef* entitles us to believe, even a physical communication of world with world which, in the dawn of the twentieth century, may transcend in sober fact the wildest dreams of all the philanthropists and the philosophers who have sought to educate humanity from Socrates to Herbert Spencer."

CHAPTER 6

AFTER THE *ASTRONEF*'S forward searchlight had flashed its farewells to the thronging, cheering crowds of Washington, her propellers began to whirl, and she swung round northward on her way to say goodbye to the Empire City.

A little before midnight her two lights flashed down over New York and Brooklyn, and were almost instantly answered by hundreds of electric beams streaming up from different parts of the Twin Cities, and from several men-of-war lying in the bay and the river.

"Goodbye for the present! Have you any messages for Mars?" flickered out from above the *Astronef*'s conning-tower.

What Uncle Sam's message was, if he had one, was never deciphered, for fifty beams began dotting and dashing at once, and the result was that nothing but a blur of many mingled rays reached the conning-tower from which Lord Redgrave and his bride were taking their last look at human habitations.

"You might have known that they would all answer at once," said Zaidie. "I suppose the news papers, of course, want interviews with the leading Martians, and the others want to know what there is to be done in the way of trade. Anyhow, it would be a feather in Uncle Sam's cap if he made the first Reciprocity Treaty with another world."

"And then proceeded to corner the commerce of the Solar System," laughed Redgrave. "Well, we'll see what can be done. Although I think, as an Englishman, I ought to look after the Open Door."

"So that the Germans could get in before you, eh? That's just like you dear, good-natured English. But look," she went on, pointing downwards, "they're signalling again, all at once this time."

Half a dozen beams shone out together from the principal newspaper offices of New York. Then simultaneously they began the dotting and dashing again. Redgrave took them down in pencil, and when the signalling had stopped he read off:

"No war. Dual Alliance climbs down. Don't like idea of *Astronef.* Cables just received. Goodbye, and good luck! Come back soon, and safe!"

"What? We have stopped the war!" exclaimed Zaidie, clasping his arm. "Well, thank God for that. How could we begin our voyage better? You remember what we were saying the other day, Lenox. If that's only true, my father somewhere knows now what a blessing he has given his brother men! We've stopped a war which might have deluged the world in blood. We've saved perhaps hundreds of thousands of lives, and kept sorrow from thousands of homes. Lenox, when we get back, you and the States and the British Government will have to build a fleet of these ships, and then the Anglo-Saxon race must say to the rest of the world—"

"The millennium has come and its presiding goddess is Zaidie Redgrave. If you don't stop fighting, disband your armies and turn your fleets into liners and cargo boats, she'll proceed to sink your ships and decimate your armies until you learn sense. Is that what you mean, dear?" laughed Redgrave, as he slipped his left hand round her waist and laid his right on the searchlight-switch to reply to the message.

"Don't be ridiculous, Lenox. Still, I suppose that is something like it. They wouldn't deserve anything else if they were fools enough to go on fighting after they knew we could wipe them out.

"Exactly. I perfectly agree with your Ladyship, but still sufficient unto the day is the Armageddon thereof. Now I suppose we'd better say goodbye and be off."

"And what a goodbye," whispered Zaidie, with an upward glance into the starlit ocean of Space which lay above and around them. "Goodbye to the world itself! Well, say it, Lenox, and let us go; I want to see what the others are like."

"Very well then; goodbye it is," he said, beginning to jerk the switch backwards and forwards with irregular motions, sending short flashes and longer beams down towards the earth.

The Empire City read the farewell message.

"Thank God for the peace. Goodbye for the present. We shall convey the joint compliments of John Bull and Uncle Sam to the peoples of the planets when we find them. Au revoir!"

The message was answered by the blaze of the concentrated searchlights from land and sea all directed on the *Astronef*. For a moment her shining shape glittered like a speck of diamond in the midst of the luminous haze far up in the sky, and then it vanished for many an anxious day from mortal sight.

A few moments later Zaidie pointed over the stern and said:

"Look, there's the moon! Just fancy—our first stopping place! Well, it doesn't look so very far off at present."

Redgrave turned and saw the pale yellow crescent of the new moon swimming high above the eastern edge of the Atlantic Ocean.

"It almost looks as if we could steer straight to it right over the water—only, of course, it wouldn't wait there for us," she went on.

"Oh, it'll be there when we want it, never fear," he laughed, "and, after all, it's only a mere matter of about two hundred and forty thousand miles away, and what's that in a trip that will cover hundreds of millions? It will just be a sort of jumping-off place into Space for us."

"Still, I shouldn't like to miss seeing it," she said. "I want to see what there is on that other side which nobody has ever seen yet, and settle that question about air and water. Won't it just be heavenly to be able to come back and tell them all about it at home? But just fancy me talking stuff like this when we are going, perhaps, to solve some of the hidden mysteries of Creation, and, may be, look upon things that human eyes were never meant to see," she went on, with a sudden change in her voice.

He felt a little shiver in the arm that was resting upon his, and his hand went down and caught hers.

"Well, we shall see a good many marvels, and, perhaps, miracles, before we come back, but why should there be anything in Creation that the eyes of created beings should not look upon? Anyhow, there's one thing we shall do I hope, we shall solve once and for all the great problem of the worlds.

"Look, for instance," he went on, turning round and pointing to the west, "there is Venus following the sun. In a few days I hope you and I will be standing on her surface, perhaps trying to talk by signs with her inhabitants, and taking photographs of her scenery. There's Mars too, that little red one up yonder. Before we come back we shall have settled a good many problems about him, too. We shall have navigated the rings of Saturn, and perhaps graphed them from his surface. We shall have crossed the bands of Jupiter, and found out whether they are clouds or not; perhaps we shall have landed on one of his moons and taken a voyage round him.

"Still, that's not the question just now, and if you are in a hurry to circumnavigate the moon we'd better begin to get a wriggle on us as they say down yonder; so come below and we'll shut up. A bit later I'll show you something that no human eyes have ever seen."

"What's that?" she asked as they turned away towards the companion ladder.

"I won't spoil it by telling you," he said, stopping at the top of the stairs and taking her by the shoulders. "By the way," he went on, "I may remind your Ladyship that you are just now drawing the last breaths of earthly air which you will taste for some time, in fact until we get back. And you may as well take your last look at earth as earth, for the next time you see it it will be a planet."

She turned to the open window and looked over into the enormous void beneath, for all this time the *Astronef* had been mounting swiftly towards the zenith.

She could see, by the growing moonlight, vast, vague shapes of land and sea. The myriad lights of New York and Brooklyn were mingled in a tiny patch of dimly luminous haze. The air about her had suddenly grown bitterly cold, and she saw that the stars and planets were shining with a brilliancy she had never seen before.

Redgrave came back to her, and laying his arm across her shoulder, said:

"Well, have you said goodbye to your native world? It is a bit solemn, isn't it, saying goodbye to a world that you have been born on; which contains everything that has made up your life, everything that is dear to you?"

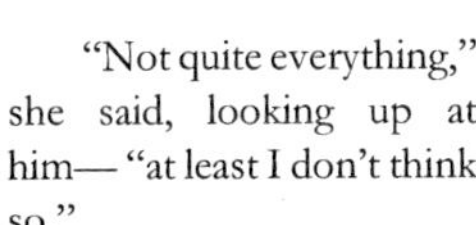

"Not quite everything," she said, looking up at him— "at least I don't think so."

He lost no time in making the only reply which was appropriate under the circumstances; and then he said, drawing her close to him:

"Nor I, as you know, darling. This is our world, a world travelling among worlds, and since I have been able to bring the most delightful of the daughters of Terra with me, I, at any rate, am perfectly happy. Now, I think it's getting on to supper time, so if your Ladyship will go to your household duties, I'll have a look at my engines and make everything snug for the voyage."

The first thing he did when he left the conning-tower was to hermetically close every external opening in the ship. Then he went and carefully inspected the apparatus for purifying the air and supplying it with fresh oxygen from the tanks in which it was stored in liquid form. Lastly he descended into the lower hold and turned on the energy of repulsion to its fullest extent, at the same time stopping the engines which had been working the propellers.

It was now no longer necessary or even possible to steer the *Astronef.* She was directed solely by the repulsive force which would carry her with ever increasing swiftness, as the attraction of the earth diminished, towards that neutral point at which the attraction of the earth is exactly balanced by the moon. Her momentum would carry her past this point, and then the "R. Force" would be gradually brought into play in order to avert the unpleasant consequences of a fall of some forty odd thousand miles.

Andrew Murgatroyd, relieved from his duties in the wheel-house, made a careful inspection of the auxiliary machinery, which was under his special charge, and then retired to his quarters in the after end of the vessel to prepare his own evening meal.

Meanwhile, her Ladyship with the help of the ingenious contrivances with which the kitchen of the *Astronef* was stocked, had prepared a dainty little Souper a deux. Her husband opened a bottle of the finest champagne that the cellars of Smeaton could supply, to drink to the prosperity of the voyage, and the health of his beautiful fellow-voyager. When he had filled the two tall glasses the wine began to run over the side which was toward the stern of the vessel. They took no notice of this at first, but when Zaidie put her glass down she stared at it for a moment, and said, in a half-frightened voice

"Why, what's the matter, Lenox? Look at the wine! It won't keep straight, and yet the table's perfectly level—and see! the water in the jug looks as though it were going to run up the side."

Redgrave took up the glass and held it balanced in his hand. When he had got the surface of the wine level the glass was no longer perpendicular to the table.

"Ah, I see what it is," he said, taking another sip and putting the glass down. "You notice that, although the wine isn't lying straight in the glass, it isn't moving about. It's just as still as it would be on earth. That means that our centre of gravity is not exactly in line with the centre of the earth. We haven't quite swung into our proper position, and that reminds me, dear. You will have to be prepared for some rather curious experiences in that way. For instance, just see if that jug of water is as heavy as it ought to be."

She took hold of the handle, and exerting, as she thought, just enough force to lift the jug a few inches, was astonished to find herself holding it out at arm's length with scarcely any effort. She put it down again very carefully as though she were afraid it would go floating off the table, and said, looking rather scared:

"That's very strange, but I suppose it's all perfectly natural?"

"Perfectly; it merely means that we have left Mother Earth a good long way behind us."

"How far?" she asked.

"I can't tell you exactly," he replied, "until I go to the instrument-room and take the angles, but I should say roughly about seventy thousand miles. When we've finished we'll go and have coffee on the upper deck, and then we shall see something of the glories of Space as no human eyes have ever seen them before."

"Seventy thousand miles away from home already, and we only started a couple of hours ago!" Zaidie found the idea a trifle terrifying, and finished her meal almost in silence. When she got up she was not a little disconcerted when the effort she made not only took her off her chair but off her feet as well. She rose into the air nearly to the surface of the table.

"Sakes!" she said, "this is getting quite a little embarrassing; I shall be hitting my head against the roof next."

"Oh, you'll soon get used to it," he laughed, pulling her down on to her feet by the skirt of her dress; "always remember to exert very little strength in everything you do, and don't forget to do everything very slowly."

When the coffee was made he carried the apparatus up into the deck-chamber. Then he came back and said:

"You'd better wrap yourself up warmly. It's a good deal colder up there than it is here."

When she reached the deck and took a first glance about her, Zaidie seemed suddenly to lapse into a state of somnambulism.

The whole heavens above and around were strewn with thick clusters of stars which she had never seen before. The stars she remembered seeing from the earth were only pin-points in the darkness compared with the myriads of blazing orbs which were now shooting their rays across the black void of Space.

So many millions of new ones had come into view, that she looked in vain for the familiar constellations. She saw only vast clusters of living gems of every colour crowding the heavens on every side of her.

She walked slowly round the deck, gazing to right and left and above, incapable for the moment either of thought or speech, but only of dumb wonder, mingled with a dim sense of overwhelming awe. Presently she craned her neck backwards and looked straight up to the zenith. A huge silver crescent, supporting, as it were, a dim greenish-coloured body in its arms, stretched overhead across nearly a sixth of the heavens.

Then Redgrave came to her side, took her in his arms, lifted her as if she had been a little child, and laid her in a long, low deck-chair, so that she could look at it without inconvenience.

The splendid crescent seemed to be growing visibly bigger, and as she lay there in a trance of wonder and admiration she saw point after point of dazzling white light flash out in the dark portions, and then begin to send out rays as though they were gigantic volcanoes in full eruption, and were pouring torrents of living fire from their blazing craters.

"Sunrise on the Moon!" said Redgrave, who had stretched himself on another chair beside her. "A glorious sight, isn't it? But nothing to what we shall see tomorrow morning—only there doesn't happen to be any morning just about here."

"Yes," she said dreamily, "glorious, isn't it? That and all the stars—but I can't think anything yet, Lenox, it's all too mighty and too marvellous. It doesn't seem as though human eyes were meant to look upon things like this But where's the earth? We must be able to see that still."

"Not from here," he said, "because it's underneath us. Come below now, and you shall see what I promised you."

They went down into the lower part of the vessel and to the after end behind the engine-room. Redgrave switched on a couple of electric lights, and then pulled a lever attached to one of the side-walls. A part of the flooring about six feet square slid noiselessly away; then he pulled another lever on the opposite side and a similar piece disappeared, leaving a large space covered only by a thick plate of absolutely transparent glass. He switched off the lights again and led her to the edge of it, and said:

"There is your native world, dear. That is your Mother Earth."

Wonderful as the moon had seemed, the gorgeous spectacle which lay seemingly at her feet was infinitely more magnificent. A vast disc of silver grey, streaked and dotted with lines and points of dazzling lights, and more than half covered with vast, glimmering, greyish-green expanses, seemed to form the floor of the tremendous gulf beneath them. They were not yet too far away to make out the general features of the continents and oceans, and fortunately the hemisphere presented to them happened to be singularly free from clouds.

To the right spread out the majestic outlines of the continents of North and South America, and to the left Asia, the Malay Archipelago, and Australia. At the top was a vast, roughly circular area of dazzling whiteness, and Redgrave, pointing to this, said:

"There, look up a little further north than the middle of that white patch, and you'll see what eyes but yours and mine have ever seen—the North Pole! When we come back we shall see the South Pole, because we shall approach the earth from the other end, as it were.

"I suppose you recognise a good deal of the picture. All that bright part up to the north, with the black spots on it, is Canada. The black spots are forests. That long white line to the left is the Rockies. You see they're all bright at the north, and as you go south you only see a few bright dots. Those are the snow-peaks.

"Those long thin white lines in South America are the tops of the Andes, and the big, dark patches to the right of them are the forests and plains of Brazil and the Argentine. Not a bad way of studying geography, is it? If we stopped here long enough we should see the whole earth spin right round under us, but we haven't time for that. We shall be in the moon before it's morning in New York, but we shall probably get a glimpse of Europe to-morrow.'

Zaidie stood gazing for nearly an hour at this marvellous vision of the home-world which she had left so far behind her before she could tear herself away and allow her husband to shut the slides again. The greatly diminished weight of her body destroyed the fatigue of standing almost entirely. In fact, on board the *Astronef* just then it was almost as easy to stand as it was to lie down.

There was of course very little sleep for the travellers on this first night of their wonderful voyage, but towards the sixth hour after leaving the earth, Zaidie, overcome as much by the emotions which had been awakened within her as by physical fatigue, went to bed, after making her husband promise that he would wake her in good time to see the descent upon the moon. Two hours later she was awake and drinking the coffee which he had prepared for her. Then she went on to the upper deck.

To her astonishment she found, on one hand, day more brilliant than she had ever seen it before, and on the other hand darkness blacker than the blackest earthly night. On the right was an intensely brilliant orb, about half as large again as the full moon seen from the earth, shining with inconceivable brightness out of a sky black as midnight and thronged with stars. It was the Sun; the Sun shining in the midst of airless Space.

The tiny atmosphere enclosed in the glass-domed deck-space was lighted brilliantly, but it was not perceptibly warmer, though Redgrave warned her not to touch anything upon which the sun's rays fell directly, as she might find it uncomfortably hot. On the other side was the same black immensity which she had seen the night before, an ocean of darkness clustered with islands of light. High above in the zenith floated the great silver-grey disc of earth, a good deal smaller now. But there was another object beneath them which was at present of far more interest to her.

Looking down to the left, she saw a vast semi-luminous area in which not a star was to be seen. It was the earth-lit portion of the long familiar and yet mysterious orb which was to be their resting place for the next few hours.

"The sun hasn't risen over there yet," said Redgrave, as she was peering down into the void. It's earth-light still. Now look at the other side."

She crossed the deck, and saw the strangest scene she had yet beheld. Apparently only a few miles below her was a huge crescent-shaped plain arching away for hundreds of miles on either side. The outer edge had a ragged look, and little excrescences, which soon took the shape of flat-topped mountains, projected from it and stood out bright and sharp against the black void beneath, out of which the stars shone up, as it seemed, a few feet beyond the edge of the disc.

The plain itself was a scene of awful and utter desolation. Huge mountain-walls, towering to immense heights and enclosing great circular and oval plains, one side of them blazing with intolerable light, and the other side black with impenetrable obscurity; enormous valleys reaching down from brilliant day into rayless night—perhaps down into the very bowels of the dead world itself; vast grey-white plains lying round the mountains, crossed by little ridges and by long black lines, which could only be immense fissures with perpendicular sides—but all hard, grey-white and black, all intolerable brightness or inky gloom; not a sign of life anywhere; no shady forests, no green fields, no broad, glittering oceans; only a ghastly wilderness of dead mountains and dead plains.

"What an awful place," Zaidie whispered. "Surely we can't land there. How far are we from it?"

"About fifteen hundred miles," replied Redgrave, who was sweeping the scene below him with one of the two powerful telescopes which stood on the deck. "No, it doesn't look very cheerful, does it? But it's a marvellous sight for all that, and one that a good many people on earth would give one of their eyes to see from here. I'm letting her drop pretty fast, and we shall probably land in a couple of hours or so. Meanwhile you may as well get out your moon atlas, and study your lunography. I'm going to turn the power a bit astern so that we shall go down obliquely, and see more of the lighted disc. We started at new moon so that you should have a look at the full earth, and also so that we could get round to the invisible side while it is lighted up." They both went below, he to deflect the repulsive force so that one set of engines should give them a somewhat oblique direction, while the other, acting directly on the surface of the moon, simply retarded their fall; and she to get out her maps.

When they got back the *Astronef* had changed her apparent position, and, instead of falling directly on to the moon, was descending towards it in a slanting direction. The result of this was that the sunlit crescent rapidly grew in breadth. Peak after peak and range after range rose up swiftly out of the black gulf beyond. The sun climbed quickly up through the star-strewn, mid-day heavens, and the full earth sank more swiftly still behind them.

Another hour of silent, entranced wonder and admiration followed, and then Redgrave said:

"Don't you think it's about time we were beginning to think of breakfast, dear—or do you think you can wait till we land?"

"Breakfast on the moon!"she exclaimed. "That would be just too lovely for words—of course we'll wait!"

"Very well," he said; "you see that big black ring nearly below us? —that, as I suppose you know, is the celebrated Mount Tycho. I'll try and find a convenient spot on the top of the ring to drop on, and then you will be able to survey the scenery from seventeen or eighteen thousand feet above the plains."

About two hours later a slight, jarring tremor ran through the frame of the vessel, and the first stage of the voyage was ended. After a passage of less than twelve hours the *Astronef* had crossed a gulf of nearly two hundred and fifty thousand miles, and rested on the untrodden surface of the lunar world.

CHAPTER 7

"WELL, MADAME, WE'VE ARRIVED. This is the moon and there is the earth. To put it into plain figures, you are now two hundred and forty thousand odd miles away from home. I think you said you would like breakfast on the surface of the World that Has Been, and so, as it's about eleven o'clock earth-time, we'll call it a dejeuner, and then we'll go and see what this poor old skeleton of a world is like."

"Oh, then we shan't actually have breakfast on the moon?"

"My dear child, of course you will. Isn't the *Astronef* resting now—right now as they say in some parts of the States on the top of the crater wall of Tycho? Aren't we really and actually on the surface of the moon? Just look at this frightful black and white, god-forsaken landscape! Isn't it like everything that you've ever learnt about the moon? Nothing but light and shade, black and white, peaks of mountains blazing in sunlight, and valleys underneath them as black as the hinges of

"—Tophet," said Zaidie, interrupting him quickly. "Yes, I see what you mean. So we'll have our dejeuner here, breathing our own nice atmosphere, and eating and drinking what was grown on the soil of dear old Mother Earth. It's a wee bit paralysing to think of, isn't it, dear? Two hundred and forty thousand miles across the gulf of Space—and we sitting here at our breakfast table just as comfortable as though we were in the Cecil in London, or the Waldorf-Astoria in New York!"

"There's nothing much in that, I mean as regards distance. You see, before we've finished we shall probably, at least I hope we shall, be eating a breakfast or a dinner together a thousand million miles or more from New York or London. Your Ladyship must remember that this is only the first stage on the journey, the jumping-off place as you called it. You see the distance from Washington to New York is—well, it isn't even a hop, skip and a jump in comparison with—"

"Oh yes, I see what you mean of course, and so I suppose I had better cut off or short-circuit such sympathies with Mother Earth as are not connected with your noble self, and get breakfast ready. How's that?"

"Well," said Lord Redgrave, looking at her as she rose from the table, "I think our honeymoon in Space is young enough yet to make it possible for me to say that your Ladyship's opinion is exactly right.

"That's a hopeless commonplace! Really, Lenox, I thought you were capable of something better than that."

"My dear Zaidie, it has been my fate to have many friends who have had honeymoons on earth, and some of their experience seems to be that the man who contradicts his wife during the first six weeks of matrimony simply makes an ass of himself. He offends her and makes himself unhappy, and it sometimes takes six months or more to get back to bearings."

"What a lot of silly men and women you must have known, Lenox. Is that the way Englishmen start marriage in England? If it is, I don't wonder at Englishmen coming across the Atlantic in liners and air-ships and so on to get American wives. I guess you can't understand your own womenfolk."

"Or perhaps they don't understand us; but anyhow, I don't think I've made any great mistake."

"No, I don't think you have. Of course if I thought so I wouldn't be here now. But this is very well for a breakfast talk; all the same, I should like to know how we are going to take the promenade you promised me on the surface of the moon?"

"Your Ladyship has only to finish her breakfast, and then everything shall be made plain to her, even the deepest craters of the mountains of the moon."

"Very well, then, I will eat swiftly and in obedience; and meanwhile, as your Lordship seems to have finished, perhaps—"

"Yes, I will go and see to the mechanical necessities," said Redgrave, swallowing his last cup of coffee, and getting up. "If you'll come down to the lower deck when you've finished, I'll have your breathing-suit ready for you, and then we'll go into the air-chamber."

"Thanks, dear, yes," she said, putting out her hand to him as he left the table, "the ante-chamber to other worlds. Isn't it just lovely? Fancy me being able to leave one world and land on another, and have you to say just those few words which make it all possible. I wonder what all the girls of all the civilised countries of earth would give just to be me right now."

"They could none of them give what you gave me, Zaidie, because you see from my point of view there's only one Zaidie in the world—or as perhaps I ought to say just now, in the Solar System."

"Very prettily said, sir!" she laughed, when she had given him his due reward for his courtly speech. "I am too dazed with all these wonders about me to—"

"To reply to it? You've given me the most convincing reply possible. Now finish your breakfast, and I'll tell you when the breathing- dresses and the air-chamber are ready. By the way, don't forget your cameras. It's quite possible we may find something worth taking pictures of, and you needn't trouble much about the weight. You know, you and I and all that we carry will only weigh about a sixth of what we did on the earth."

"Very well, then, I'll take the whole-plate apparatus as well as the Kodak and the panorama camera. When I'm ready, Murgatroyd will tell you to come down."

"But isn't he coming with us too?"

"My dear girl, if I were to ask Murgatroyd to leave the *Astronef* there'd be a mutiny on board—a mutiny of one against one. No, he's left his native world; but he says he's done it in a ship that's made with British steel out of English iron mines, smelted, forged and fashioned in English works, and so to him it's a bit of England, however far away from Mother Earth it may be; and if you ever see Andrew Murgatroyd's big head and good, ungainly body outside the *Astronef* in any of the worlds, dead or alive, that we're going to visit—well, when we get back to Mother Earth you may ask me—"

"I don't think I'll have to ask you for anything, Lenox. I believe if I wanted anything you'd know before I did, so go away and get those breathing-dresses ready. I didn't come to the moon to talk commonplaces with a husband I've been married to for nearly three days."

"Is it really as long as that?"

"Oh, don't be ridiculous, even if you are beyond the limits of earthly conventionalities. Anyhow, I've been married long enough to want my own way, and just now I want a promenade on the moon."

"The will of her Ladyship is a law unto her servant, and that which she hath said shall be done! If you come down on to the lower deck in ten minutes everything shall be ready."

With this he disappeared down the companion-way.

About five minutes afterwards Andrew Murgatroyd showed his grizzled, long-bearded face with its high forehead, heavy brows, and broad-set eyes, long nose and shaven upper lip, just above the stairway and said, for all the world as though he might have been giving out the number of the hymn in his beloved Ebenezer at Smeaton:

"If it pleases yer Ladyship, his Lordship is ready, and if you'll please come down I'll show you the way."

"Oh, thank you, Mr. Murgatroyd!" said Zaidie, getting up and going towards the companion-way; "but I'm afraid you don't think that—I mean you don't seem to take very much interest—"

"If your Ladyship will pardon me," said the old man, standing aside to let her go down, "it is not my business to think on board his Lordship's vessel. I am his servant, and my fathers have been his fathers' servants for more years than I'd like to count. If it wasn't that way I wouldn't be here. Will your Ladyship please to come down?"

Zaidie bowed her beautiful head in recognition of this ages-old devotion, and said as she passed him, more sweetly than he had ever heard human lips speak:

"Thank you, Mr. Murgatroyd. You've taught me something in those few words that we have no knowledge of in the States. Good service is as honourable as good mastership. Thank you."

Murgatroyd put up his lower lip and half smiled with his upper, for he was not yet quite sure of this radiant beauty, who, according to his ideas, should have been English and wasn't. Then, with a rather clumsy and yet eloquent gesture, he showed her the way down to the air-chamber.

She nodded to him with a smile as she passed in through the air-tight door, and when she heard the levers swing to and the bolts shoot into their places she felt as though, for the time being, she had said goodbye to a friend.

Her husband was waiting for her almost fully clad in his breathing-dress. He had hers all ready to put on, and when the necessary changes and investments had been made, Zaidie found herself clad in a costume which was not by any means unlike the diving-dresses of common use, save that they were very much lighter in construction.

The helmets were smaller, and not having to withstand outside pressure they were made of welded aluminium, lined thickly with asbestos, not to keep the cold out, but the heat in. On the back of the dress there was a square case, looking like a knap-sack, containing the expanding apparatus, which would furnish breathable air for an almost unlimited time as long as the liquefied air from a cylinder hung below it passed through the cells in which the breathed air had been deprived of its carbonic acid gas and other noxious ingredients.

The pressure of air inside the helmet automatically regulated the supply, which was not permitted to circulate through the other portions of the dress, The reasons for this precaution were very simple. Granted the absence of atmosphere on the moon, any air in the dress, which was woven of a cunning compound of silk and asbestos, would instantly expand with irresistible force, burst the covering, and expose the limbs of the explorers to a cold which would be infinitely more destructive than the hottest of earthly fires. It would wither them to nothing in a moment.

A human hand or foot—we won't say anything about faces exposed to the summer or winter temperature of the moon—that is to say, to its sunlight and its darkness—would be shrivelled into dry bone in a moment, and therefore Lord Redgrave, foreseeing this, had provided the breathing-dresses. Lastly, the two helmets were connected, for purposes of conversation by a light wire, the two ends of which were connected with a little telephonic receiver and transmitter inside each of the head-dresses.

"Well, now I think we're ready," said Redgrave, putting his hand on the lever which opened the outer door.

His voice sounded a little queer and squeaky over the wire, and for the matter of that so did Zaidie's as she replied:

"Yes, I'm ready, I think. I hope these things will work all right."

"You may be quite sure that I shouldn't have put you into one of them if I hadn't tested them pretty thoroughly," he replied, swinging the door open and throwing out a light folding iron ladder which was hinged to the floor.

They were in the shade cast by the hull of the *Astronef*. For about ten yards in front of her Zaidie saw a dense black shadow, and beyond it a stretch of grey-white sand lit up by a glare of sunlight which would have been intolerable if it had not been for the smoke-coloured slips of glass which had been fitted behind the glass visors of the helmets.

Over it were thickly scattered boulders and pieces of rock bleached and desiccated, and each throwing a black shadow, fantastically shaped and yet clearly defined on the grey-white sand behind it. There was no soil, and all the softer kind of rock and stone had crumbled away ages ago. Every particle of moisture had long since evaporated; even chemical combinations had been dissolved by the alternations of heat and cold known only on earth to the chemist in his laboratory.

Only the hardest rocks, such as granites and basalts, remained. Everything else had been reduced to the universal grey-white impalpable powder into which Zaidie's shoes sank when she, holding her husband's hand, went down the ladder and stood at the foot of it—first of the earth-dwellers to set foot on another world.

Redgrave followed her with a little spring from the centre of the ladder which landed him with strange gentleness beside her. He took both her gloved hands and pressed them hard in his. He would have kissed his welcome to the World that Had Been if he could, but that of course was out of the question, and so he had to be content with telling her that he wanted to.

Then, hand in hand, they crossed the little plateau towards the edge of the tremendous gulf, fifty-four miles across and nearly twenty thousand feet deep, which forms the crater of Tycho. In the middle of it rose a conical mountain about five thousand feet high, the summit of which was just beginning to catch the solar rays. Half of the vast plain was already brilliantly illuminated, but round the central cone was a semicircle of shadow of impenetrable blackness.

"Day and night in this same valley, actually side by side!" said Zaidie. Then she stopped and pointed down into the brightly lit distance, and went on hurriedly, "Look, Lenox; look at the foot of the mountain there! Doesn't that seem like the ruins of a city?"

"It does," he said, "and there's no reason why it shouldn't be. I've always thought that, as the air and water disappeared from the upper parts of the moon, the inhabitants, whoever they were, must have been driven down into the deeper parts. Shall we go down and see?"

"But how?" she said.

He pointed towards the *Astronef*. She nodded her helmeted head, and they went back towards the vessel.

A few minutes later the Space-Navigator had risen from her resting-place with an impetus which rapidly carried her over half of the vast crater, and then she began to drop slowly into the depths. She grounded gently, and presently they were standing on the ground about a mile from the central cone. This time, however, Redgrave had taken the precaution to bring a magazine rifle and a couple of revolvers with him in case any strange monsters, relics of the vanished fauna of the moon, might still be taking refuge in these mysterious depths. Zaidie, although like a good many American girls she could shoot excellently well, carried no weapon more offensive than the photographic apparatus aforesaid.

The first thing that Redgrave did when they stepped out on to the sandy surface of the plain was to stoop down and strike a wax match. There was a tiny glimmer of light, which was immediately extinguished.

"No air here," he said, "so we shall find no living beings—at any rate, none like ourselves."

They found the walking exceedingly easy, although their boots were purposely weighted in order to counteract, to some extent, the great difference in gravity. A few minutes brought them to the outskirts of the city. It had no walls and exhibited no signs of any devices for defence. Its streets were broad and well-paved, and the houses, built of great blocks of grey stone joined together with white cement, looked as fresh and unworn as though they had only been built a few months, whereas they had probably stood for hundreds of thousands of years. They were flat-roofed, all of one storey and practically of one type.

There were very few public buildings, and absolutely no attempt at ornamentation was visible. Round some of the houses were spaces which might once have been gardens. In the midst of the city, which appeared to cover an area of about four square miles, was an enormous square paved with flag-stones, which were covered to the depth of a couple of inches with a light grey dust, which, as they walked across it, remained perfectly still save for the disturbance caused by their footsteps. There was no air to support it, otherwise it might have risen in clouds about them.

From the centre of this square rose a huge pyramid nearly a thousand feet in height, the sole building of the great silent city which appeared to have been raised most probably as a temple by the hands of its long-dead inhabitants.

When they got nearer they saw a white fringe round the steps by which it was approached, and they soon found that this fringe was composed of millions of white-bleached bones and skulls, shaped very much like those of terrestrial men, save that they were

very much larger, and that the ribs were out of all proportion to the rest of the skeleton. They stopped awe-stricken before this strange spectacle. Redgrave stooped down and took hold of one of the bones, a huge femur. It broke in two as he tried to lift it, and the piece which remained in his hand crumbled instantly to white powder.

"Whoever they were," he said, "they were giants. When air and water failed above, they came down here by some means and built this city. You see what enormous chests they must have had. That would be Nature's last struggle to enable them to breathe the diminishing atmosphere. These, of course, were the last descendants of the fittest to breathe it; this was their temple, I suppose, and here they came to die—I wonder how many thousand years ago—perishing of heat, and cold, and hunger, and thirst; the last tragedy of a race, which, after all, must have been something like ourselves."

"It's just too awful for words," said Zaidie. "Shall we go into the temple? That seems one of the entrances up there, only I don't like walking over all those bones."

"I don't suppose they'll mind if we do," replied Redgrave, "only we mustn't go far in. It may be full of cross passages and mazes, and we might never get out. Our lamps won't be much use in there, you know, for there's no air. They'll just be points of light, and we shan't see anything but them. It's very aggravating, but I'm afraid there's no help for it. Come along."

They ascended the steps, crushing the bones and skulls to powder beneath their feet, and entered the huge, square doorway, which looked like a rectangle of blackness against the grey-white of the wall. Even through their asbestos-woven clothing they felt a sudden shock of icy cold. In those few steps they had passed from a temperature of tenfold summer heat into one below that of the coldest spots on earth They turned on the electric lamps which were fitted to the breastplates of their dresses, but they could see nothing save the thin thread of light straight in front of them. It did not even spread. It was like a polished needle on a background of black velvet.

All about them was darkness impenetrable, and so they reluctantly turned back to the doorway, leaving all the mysteries which that vast temple of a long-vanished people might contain to remain mysteries to the end of time.

They passed down the steps again and crossed the square, and for the next half-hour Zaidie was busy taking photographs of the pyramid with its ghastly surroundings, and a few general views of this strange City of the Dead.

CHAPTER 8

WHEN THEY GOT BACK they found Murgatroyd pacing up and down the floor of the deck-chamber, looking about him with serious eyes, but betraying no other visible sign of anxiety. The *Astronef* was at once his home and his idol, and, as Redgrave had said, even his own direct orders would hardly have induced him to leave her even in a world in which there was not a living human being to dispute possession of her.

When they had resumed their ordinary clothing the *Astronef* rose from the surface of the plain, crossed the encircling wall at the height of a few hundred feet, and made her way at a speed of about fifty miles an hour towards the regions of the South Pole.

Behind them to the north-west they could see from their elevation of nearly thirty thousand feet the vast expanse of the Sea of Clouds. Dotted here and there were the shining points and ridges of light marking the peaks and crater-walls which the rays of the rising sun had already touched. Before them and to the right and left rose a vast maze of ragged, splintery peaks and huge ramparts of mountain-walls enclosing plains so far below their summits that the light of neither sun nor earth ever reached them.

By directing the force exerted by what might now be called the propelling part of the engines against the mountain masses which they crossed to right and left and behind, Redgrave was able to take a zigzag course that carried them over many of the walled plains which were wholly or partially lit up by the sun, and in nearly all of the deepest their telescopes revealed something like what they had found within the crater of Tycho. At length, pointing to a gigantic circle of white light fringing an abyss of utter darkness, he said:" There is Newton, the greatest mystery of the moon. Those inner walls are twenty-four thousand feet high; that means that the bottom, which has never been seen by human eyes, is about five thousand feet below the surface of the moon. What do you say, dear—shall we go down and see if the searchlight will show us anything? You know there may be something like breathable air down there, and perhaps living creatures who call breathe it."

"Certainly!" replied Zaidie decisively; "haven't we come to see things that nobody else has ever seen?"

Redgrave went down to the engine-room, and presently the *Astronef* changed her course, and in a few minutes was hanging with her polished hull bathed in sunlight, like a star suspended over the unfathomable gulf of darkness below.

As they sank below the level of the sun-rays, Murgatroyd turned on both the searchlights. They dropped down ever slowly and more slowly until gradually the two long, thin streams of light began to spread themselves out; the lower they went the more the beams spread out, and by the time the *Astronef* came gently to a rest they were swinging round her in broad fans of diffused light over a dark, marshy surface, with scattered patches of grey moss and reeds, with dull gleams of stagnant water showing between them.

"Air and water at last! I thought so," said Redgrave, as he rejoined her on the upper deck; "air and water and eternal darkness! Well, we shall find life on the moon here if anywhere."

"I suppose we had better put on our breathing-dresses, hadn't we?" asked Zaidie.

"Certainly," he replied, "because, although there is some sort of air, we don't know yet whether we shall be able to breathe it. It may be half carbon dioxide for all we know; but a few matches will soon tell us that."

Within a quarter of an hour they were again standing on the surface. Murgatroyd had orders to follow them as far as possible with the head searchlight, which, in the comparatively rarefied atmosphere, appeared to have a range of several miles. Redgrave struck a match, and held it up level with his head; it burnt with a clear, steady, yellow flame.

"Where a match will burn a man should be able to breathe," he said. "I'm going to see what lunar air is like."

"For Heaven's sake be careful, dear," came the reply in pleading tones across the wire.

"All right; but don't open your helmet until I tell you."

He then raised the hermetically closed slide of glass, which formed the front of the helmets, half an inch or so. Instantly he felt a sensation like the drawing of a red-hot iron across his skin. He snapped the visor down and clasped it in its place. For a moment or two he gasped for breath, and then he said rather faintly:

"It's no good, it's too cold. It would freeze the blood of a salamander. I think we'd better go back and explore this place under cover. We can't do anything in the dark, and we can see just as well from the upper deck with the searchlights. Besides, as there's air and water here, there's no telling but there may be inhabitants of sorts such as we shouldn't care to meet."

He took her hand, and to Murgatroyd's great relief they went back to the vessel.

Redgrave then raised the *Astronef* a couple of hundred feet and, by directing the repulsive force against the mountain walls, developed just sufficient energy to keep them moving at about twelve miles an hour.

They began to cross the plain with their searchlights flashing out in all directions. They had scarcely gone a mile before the head-light fell upon a moving form half walking, half crawling among some stunted brown-leaved bushes by the side of a broad, stagnant stream.

"Look!" said Zaidie, clasping his arm, "is that a gorilla, or—no, it can't be a man."

The light was turned full upon the object. If it had been covered with hair it might have passed for some strange type of the ape tribe, hut its skin was smooth and of a livid grey. Its lower limbs were evidently more powerful than its upper; its chest was enormously developed, but the stomach was small. The head was big and round and smooth. As they came nearer they saw that in place of fingernails it had long white feelers which it kept extended and constantly waving about as it groped its way towards the water. As the intense light flashed full on it, it turned its head towards them. It had a nose and a mouth—the nose, long and thick, with huge mobile nostrils; the mouth forming an angle something like a fish's lips. Teeth there seemed none. At either side of the upper part of the nose there were two little sunken holes—in which this thing's ancestors of countless thousands of years ago had once had eyes.

As she looked upon this awful parody of what had once perhaps been a human face, Zaidie covered hers with her hands and uttered a little moan of horror.

"Horrible, isn't it?" said Redgrave. "I suppose that's what the last remnants of the Lunarians have come to. Evidently once men and women, something like ourselves. I daresay the ancestors of that thing have lived here in coldness and darkness for hundreds of generations. It shows how tremendously tenacious Nature is of life.

"Ages ago, no doubt, that brute's ancestors lived up yonder when there were seas and rivers, fields and forests, just as we have them on earth, among men and women who could see and breathe and enjoy everything in life and had built up civilisations like ours!

"Look, it's going to fish or something. Now we shall see what it feeds on. I wander why the water isn't frozen. I suppose there must be some internal heat left still. A few patches with lakes of lava under them. Perhaps this valley is just over one, and that's why these creatures have managed to survive.

"Ah! there's another of them, smaller, not so strongly formed. That thing's mate, I suppose-female of the species. Ugh! I wonder how many hundred of thousands of years it will take for our descendants to come to that."

"I hope our dear old earth will hit something else and be smashed to atoms before that happens!" exclaimed Zaidie, whose curiosity had now partly overcome her horror. "Look, it's trying to catch something!"

The larger of the two creatures had groped its way to the edge of the sluggish, oily water and dropped, or rather rolled, quietly into it. It was evidently cold-blooded, or nearly so, for no warm-blooded animal would have taken to such water so naturally. Presently the other dropped in too, and both disappeared for some moments. Then, in the midst of a violent commotion in the water a few yards away, they rose to the surface of the water, the larger with a wriggling, eel-like fish between its jaws.

They both groped their way towards the edge, and had just reached it and were pulling themselves out when a hideous shape rose out of the water behind them. It was like the head of an octopus joined to the body of a boa-constrictor, but head and neck were both of the same ghastly, livid grey as the other two creatures. It was evidently blind, too, for it took no notice of the brilliant glare of the searchlight, but it moved rapidly towards the two scrambling forms, its long white feelers trembling out in all directions. Then one of them touched the smaller of the two shapes. Instantly the rest shot out and closed round it, and with scarcely a struggle it was dragged beneath the water and vanished.

Zaidie uttered a little low scream and covered her face again, and Redgrave said:

"The same old brutal law you see, life preying upon life even on a dying world, a world that is more than half dead itself. Well, I think we've seen enough of this place. I suppose those arc about the only types of life we should meet anywhere, and I don't want to know much more about them. I vote we go and see what the invisible hemisphere is like."

"I have had all I want of this side," said Zaidie, looking away from the scene of the hideous tragedy, "so the sooner we go, the better I shall like it."

A few minutes later the *Astronef* was again rising towards the stars with her searchlights still flashing down into the Valley of Expiring Life, which had seemed to them even worse than the Valley of Death. As he followed the rays with a pair of powerful field glasses, Redgrave fancied that he saw huge, dim shapes moving about the stunted shrubbery and through the slimy pools of the stagnant rivers, and once or twice he got a glimpse of what might well have been the ruins of towns and cities, hut the gloom soon

became too deep and dense for the searchlights to pierce and he was glad when the *Astronef* soared up into the brilliant sunlight once more. Even the ghastly wilderness of the lunar landscape was welcome after the nameless horrors of that hideous abyss.

After a couple of hours' rapid travelling, Redgrave pointed down to a comparatively small, deep crater, and said:

"There, this is Malapert. It is almost exactly at the south pole of the moon, and there," he went on, pointing ahead, "is the horizon of the hemisphere. which no earthborn eyes have ever seen."

"Except ours," said Zaidie somewhat inconsequently, "and I wonder what we shall see."

"Probably something very like what we have seen on this side," replied Redgrave, and as the event proved, he was right.

Contrary to many ingenious speculations which have been indulged in by both scientist and romancer, they found that the hemisphere, which for countless ages had never been turned towards the earth, was almost an exact replica of the visible one. Fully three-fourths of it was brilliantly illuminated by the Sun, and what they saw through their glasses was practically the same as what they had beheld on the earthward side; huge groups of enormous craters and ringed mountains, long, irregular chains crowned with sharp, splintery peaks, and between these vast, deeply depressed areas, ranging in colour from dazzling white to grey-brown, marking the beds of the vanished lunar seas.

As they crossed one of these, Redgrave allowed the *Astronef* to sink to within a few thousand feet of the surface, and then he and Zaidie swept it with their telescopes. Their chance search was rewarded by something they had not seen in the sea-beds of the other hemisphere.

These depressions were far deeper than the others, evidently many thousands of feet below the average surface, but the sun's rays were blazing full into this one, and, dotted round its slopes at varying elevations, they made out little patches which seemed to differ from the general surface.

"I wonder if those are the remains of cities," said Zaidie. "Isn't it possible that the old peoples of the moon might have built their cities along the seas just as we do, and that their descendants may have followed the waters as they retreated, I mean as they either dried up or disappeared into the centre?"

"Very probable indeed, dearest of philosophers," he said, picking her up with one arm and kissing the smiling lips which had just uttered this most reasonable deduction. "Now we'll go down and see."

He diminished the vertically repulsive force a little, and the *Astronef* dropped slantingly towards the bed of what might once have been the Pacific of the Moon.

When they were within about a couple of thousand feet of the surface it became perfectly plain that Zaidie was correct in her hypothesis. The vast sea floor was thickly strewn with the ruins of countless cities and towns, which had been inhabited by an equally countless series of generations of men and women, who had perhaps lived and loved in the days when our own world was a glowing mass of molten rock, surrounded by the envelope of vapours which has since condensed to form our oceans.

They dropped still lower and ran diagonally across the ocean-bed, and as they did so Zaidie's proposition was more and more completely confirmed, for they saw that the towns and cities which stood highest were the most dilapidated, and that the buildings had evidently been torn and crumbled away by the action of wind and water, snow and ice.

The nearer they approached to the central and deepest depression, the better preserved and the simpler the buildings became, until down in the lowest depths they found a collection of low-built square edifies, scarcely better than huts, which had clustered round the little lake into which, ages before, the ocean had dwindled. But where the lake had been there was now only a shallow depression covered with grey sand and brown rock.

Into this they descended and touched the lunar surface for the last time. A couple of hours' excursion among the houses proved that they had been the last refuge of the last descendants of a dying race, a race which had socially degenerated just as the succession of cities had done architecturally, age by age, as the long-drawn struggle for mere existence had become keener and keener until the two last essentials, air and water, had failed—and then the end had come.

The streets, like the square of the great Temple of Tycho, were strewn with myriads and myriads of bones, and there were myriads more scattered round what had once been the shores of the dwindling lake. Here, as elsewhere, there was not a sign or a record of any kind—carving or sculpture. If there were any such on the surface of the moon they had not discovered them. The buildings which they had seen evidently belonged to the decadent period during which the dwindling remnants of the Selenites asked only to eat and drink and breathe.

Inside the great Pyramid of the City of Tycho they might, perhaps, have found something—some stone or tablet which bore the mark of the artist's hand; elsewhere, perhaps, they might have found cities reared by older races, which might have rivalled the creations of Egypt and Babylon, but they had neither time nor inclination to look for these.

All that they had seen of the Dead World had only sickened and saddened them. The untravelled regions of Space peopled by living worlds more akin to their own were before them. The red disc of Mars was glowing in the zenith among the diamond-white clusters which gemmed the black sky behind him.

More than a hundred millions of miles had to be traversed before they would be able to set foot on his surface, and so, after one last look round the Valley of Death about them, Redgrave turned on the full energy of the repulsive force in a vertical direction, and the *Astronef* leapt upwards in a straight line for her new destination. The Unknown Hemisphere spread out in a vast plain beneath them, the blazing sun rose on their left, and the brilliant silver orb of the earth on their right, and so, full of wonder and yet without regret, they bade farewell to the World that Had Been.

CHAPTER 8

THE EARTH AND THE MOON were more than a hundred million miles behind in the depths of Space, and the *Astronef* had crossed this immense gap in eleven days and a few hours; but this apparently inconceivable speed was not altogether due to the powers of the Navigator of the Stars, for Lord Redgrave had taken advantage of the passage of the planet along its orbit towards that of the earth; therefore, while the *Astronef* was approaching Mars with ever-increasing speed, Mars was travelling towards the *Astronef* at the rate of sixteen miles a second.

The great silver disc of the earth had diminished until it looked only a little larger than Venus appears from the earth. In fact the planet Terra is to the inhabitants of Mars what Venus is to us, the star of the morning and evening.

Breakfast on the morning of the twelfth day—or, since there is neither day nor night in Space, it would be more correct to say the twelfth period of twenty-four earth-hours as measured by the chronometers—was just over, and Redgrave was standing with his bride in the forward end of the deck-chamber looking downwards at a vast crescent of rosy light which stretched out over an arc of more than ninety degrees. Two tiny black spots were travelling towards each other across it.

"Ah!" she said, going towards one of the telescopes, "there are the moons. I was reading my Gulliver last night. I wonder what the old Dean would have given to be here, and see how true his guess was. Are we going to land on them?"

"I don't see why we shouldn't," he said. "I think we might find them convenient stopping-places; besides, you know that this isn't only a pleasure-trip. We have to add as much as we can to the sum of human knowledge, and so of course we shall have to find out whether the moons of Mars have atmospheres and inhabitants."

"What, people living on those wee things?" she laughed, "why, they're only about thirty or forty miles round, aren't they?"

"About," he said, "but that's just one of the points I want to solve; and as for life, it doesn't always mean people, you know. We are only a few hundred miles away from Deimos, the outer one, and he is twelve thousand five hundred miles from Mars. I vote we drop on him first and let him carry us towards Phobos. And then when we've examined him we'll pay a visit to his brother and take a trip round Mars on him. Phobos does the journey in about seven hours and a half, and as he's only three thousand seven hundred miles above the surface, we ought to get a very good view of our next stopping-place."

"That ought to be quite delightful," said Zaidie, "but how commonplace you are getting, Lenox. That's so like you Englishmen. We are doing what has only been dreamt of before, and here you are talking about moons and planets as if they were railway stations."

"Well, if your ladyship prefers it, we will call them undiscovered islands and continents in the Ocean of Space. That does sound a little bit better, doesn't it? Now I must go down and see to my engines."

When he had gone, Zaidie sat down to the telescope again and kept it focussed on one of the little black spots travelling across the crescent of Mars. Both it and the other spot rapidly grew larger, and the features of the planet itself became more distinct. Soon even with her unaided eyes she could make out the seas and continents and the mysterious canals quite plainly through the clear, rosy atmosphere, and, with the aid of the telescope, she could even make out the glimmering twilight which the inner moon threw upon the unlighted portion of the planet's disc.

Deimos grew bigger and bigger, and in about half an hour the *Astronef* grounded gently on what looked to Zaidie like a dimly lighted circular plain, but which, when her eyes became accustomed to the light, was more like the summit of a conical mountain. Redgrave raised the keel a little from the surface again and steered towards a thin circle of light on the tiny horizon.

As they crossed into the sunlit portion it became quite plain that Deimos, at any rate, was as airless and lifeless as the moon. The surface was composed of brown rock and red sand broken up into miniature hills and valleys. There were a few traces of byegone volcanic action, but it was evident that the internal fires of this tiny world must have burnt themselves out very quickly.

"Not much to be seen here," said Redgrave as he came up the companion way, "and I don't think it would be safe to go out. The attraction is so weak here that we might find ourselves falling off with very little exertion. Still, you may as well take a couple of photographs of the surface, and then we'll be off to Phobos."

Zaidie got her apparatus to work, and when she had taken her slides down to the dark-room, Redgrave turned the R. Force on very slightly and Phobos began to sink away beneath them. The attraction of Mars now began to make itself strongly felt, and the *Astronef* dropped rapidly through the eight thousand miles which separate the inner and outer satellites.

As they approached Phobos they saw that half the little disc was brilliantly lighted by the same rays of the sun which were glowing on the rapidly increasing crescent of Mars beneath them. By careful manipulation of his engines Lord Redgrave managed to meet the approaching satellite with a hardly perceptible shock about the centre of its lighted portion, that is to say the side turned towards the planet.

Mars now appeared as a gigantic rosy moon filling the whole vault of the heavens above them. Their telescopes brought the three thousand seven hundred and fifty miles down to about fifty. The rapid motion of the tiny satellite afforded them a spectacle which might be compared to the rising of a moon glowing with rosy light and hundreds of times larger than the earth. The speed of the vehicle of which they had taken possession, something like four thousand two hundred miles an hour, caused the surface of the planet to apparently sweep away from below them, just as the earth appears to slip away from under the car of a balloon.

Neither of them left the telescopes for more than a few minutes during this aerial circumnavigation. Murgatroyd, outwardly impassive, but inwardly filled with solemn fears for the fate of this impiously daring voyage, brought them wine and sandwiches, and later on tea and toast and more sandwiches; but they took no moment's heed of these, so absorbed were they in the wonderful spectacle which was swiftly passing under their eyes.

The main armament of the *Astronef* consisted of four pneumatic guns, which could be mounted on swivels, two ahead and two astern, which carried a shell containing either one of two kinds of explosives invented by her creator.

One of these was a solid, and burst on impact with an explosive force equal to about twenty pounds of lyddite. The other consisted of two liquids separated by a partition in the shell, and these, when mixed by the breaking of the partition, burst into a volume of flame which could not be extinguished by any known human means. It would burn even in a vacuum, since it supplied its own elements of combustion. The guns would throw these shells to a distance of about seven terrestrial miles. On the upper deck there were also stands for a couple of light machine guns capable of discharging seven hundred explosive bullets a minute.

Professor Rennick, although a man of peace, had little sympathy with the laws of "civilised" warfare which permit men to be blown into rags of flesh and splinters of bone by explosive shells of a pound weight and upwards, and only allow projectiles of less weight to be used against "savages". He believed that when war was necessary it had to be war—and the sooner it was over the better for everybody concerned.

The small arms consisted of a couple of heavy ten-bore elephant guns carrying three-ounce melinite shells; a dozen rifles and fowling pieces of different makes of which three, a single and a double-barrelled rifle and a double-barrelled shot-gun, belonged to her ladyship, as well as a dainty brace of revolvers, one of half-a-dozen brace of various calibres which completed the minor armament of the *Astronef.*

The guns were got up and mounted while the attraction of the planet was comparatively feeble, and the guns themselves therefore of very little weight. On the surface of the earth a score of men could not have done the work, but on board the *Astronef*, suspended in space, her crew of three found the work easy. Zaidie herself picked up a Maxim and carried it about as though it were a toy sewing-machine.

"Now I think we can go down." said Redgrave, when everything had been put in position as far as possible. "I wonder whether we shall find the atmosphere of Mars suitable for terrestrial lungs. It will be rather awkward if it isn't."

A very slight exertion of repulsive force was sufficient to detach the *Astronef* from the body of Phobos. She dropped rapidly towards the surface of the planet, and within three hours they saw the sunlight, for the first time since they had left the Earth, shining through an unmistakable atmosphere, an atmosphere of a pale, rosy hue, instead of the azure of the earthly skies. An angular observation showed that they were within fifty miles of the surface of the undiscovered world.

"Well, we shall find air here of some sort, there's no doubt. We'll drop a bit further and then Andrew shall start the propellers. They'll very soon give us an idea of the density. Do you notice the change in the temperature? That's the diffused rays instead of the direct ones. Twenty miles! think that will do. I'll stop her now and we'll prospect for a landing-place."

He went down to apply the repulsive force directly to the surface of Mars, so as to check the descent, and then he put on his breathing-dress, went into the exit-chamber, closed one door behind him, opened the other and allowed it to fill with Martian air; then he shut it again, opened his visor and took a cautious breath.

It may, perhaps, have been the idea that he, the first of all the sons of Earth, was breathing the air of another world, or it might have been some property peculiar to the Martian atmosphere, but he immediately experienced a sensation such as usually follows the drinking of a glass of champagne. He took another breath, and another, then he opened the inner door and went back to the lower deck, saying to himself: "Well, the air's all right if it is a bit champagney, rich in oxygen, I suppose, with perhaps a trace of nitrous-oxide in it. Still, it's certainly breathable and that's the principal thing.

"It's all right, dear," he said as he reached the upper deck where Zaidie was walking about round the sides of the glass dome gazing with all her eyes at the strange scene of mingled cloud and sea and land which spread for an immense distance on all sides of them. "I have breathed the air of Mars, and even at this height it is distinctly wholesome, though of course it's rather thin, and I had it mixed with some of our own atmosphere. Still I think it will agree all right with us lower down."

"Well, then," said Zaidie, "suppose we get down below those clouds and see what there really is to be seen."

"As there's a fairly big problem to be solved shortly I'll see to the descent myself," he replied, going towards the stair-way.

In a couple of minutes she saw the cloud belt below them rising rapidly. When Redgrave returned the *Astronef* was plunging into a sea of rosy mist.

"The clouds of Mars," she exclaimed, "fancy a world with pink clouds! I wonder what there is on the other side."

The next moment they saw. Just below them, at a distance of about five earth-miles, lay an irregularly triangular island, a detached portion of the Continent of Huygens almost equally divided by the Martian equator, and lying with another almost similarly shaped island between the fortieth and fiftieth meridians of west longitude. The two islands were divided by a broad, straight stretch of water about the width of the English Channel between Folkestone and Boulogne. Instead of the bright blue-green of terrestrial seas, this connecting link between the great Northern and Southern Martian oceans had an orange tinge.

The land immediately beneath them was of a gently undulating character, something like the Downs of South-Eastern England. No mountains were visible in any direction. The lower portions, particularly along the borders of the canals and the sea, were thickly dotted with towns and cities, apparently of enormous extent. To the north of the Island Continent there was a peninsula, which was covered with a vast collection of buildings, which, with the broad streets and spacious squares which divided them, must have covered an area of something like two hundred square miles.

"There's the London of Mars!" said Redgrave, pointing down towards it; "where the London of Earth will be in a few thousand years, close to the equator. And you see, all those other towns and cities crowded round the canals! I daresay when we go across the northern and southern temperate zones we shall find them in about the state that Siberia or Patagonia are in."

"I dare say we shall," replied Zaidie, "Martian civilisation is crowding towards the equator, though I should call that place down there the greater New York of Mars, and—see—there's Brooklyn just across the canal. I wonder what they're thinking about us down there."

Phobos revolves from west to east almost along the plane of the planet's equator. To left and right they saw the huge ice-caps of the South and North Poles gleaming through the red atmosphere with a pale sunset glimmer. Then came the great stretches of sea, often obscured by vast banks of clouds, which, as the sunlight fell upon them, looked strangely like the earth-clouds at sunset.

Then, almost immediately underneath them, spread out the great land areas of the equatorial region. The three continents of

Halle, Gallileo, and Tycholand; then Huygens—which is to Mars what Europe, Asia, and Africa are to the earth, then Herschell and Copernicus. Nearly all of these land masses were split up into semi-regular divisions by the famous canals which have so long puzzled terrestrial observers.

"Well, there is one problem solved at any rate," said Redgrave, when after a journey of nearly four hours they had crossed the western hemisphere. "Mars is getting, very old, her seas are diminishing, and her continents are increasing. Those canals are the remains of gulfs and straits which have been widened and deepened and lengthened by human, or I should say Martian, labour, partly, I've no doubt, for purposes of navigation, and partly to keep the inhabitants of the interior of the continent within measurable distance of the sea. There's not the slightest doubt about that. Then, you see, there are scarcely any mountains to speak of so far, only ranges of low hills."

"And that means, I suppose," said Zaidie. "that they've all been worn down as the mountains of the earth are being. I was reading Flammarion's 'End of the World' last night, and he, you know, describes the earth at the last as just one big plain of land, no hills or mountains, no seas, and only sluggish rivers draining into marshes.

"I suppose that's what they're coming to down yonder. Now, I wonder what sort of civilisation we shall find. Perhaps we shan't find any at all. Suppose all their civilisations have worn out, and they are degenerating into the same struggle for sheer existence those poor creatures in the moon must have had."

"Or suppose," said his lordship rather seriously, "we find that they have passed the zenith of civilisation, and are dropping back into savagery, but still have the use of weapons and means of destruction which we, perhaps, have no notion of, and are inclined to use them. We'd better be careful, dear."

"What do you mean, Lenox?" she said. "They wouldn't try to do us any harm, would they? Why should they?"

"I don't say they would" he replied, "but still you never know. You see, their ideas of right and wrong and hospitality and all that sort of thing might quite different to what we have on the earth. In fact, they may not be men at all, but just a sort of monster with perhaps a superhuman intellect, with all sorts of extra-human ideas in it.

"Then there's another thing," he went on. "Suppose they fancied a trip through Space, and thought that they had as good a right to the *Astronef* as we have? I daresay they've seen us by this time if they've got telescopes, as no doubt they have, perhaps a good deal more powerful than ours, and they may be getting ready to receive us now. I think I'll get the guns in place before we go down, in case their moral ideas, as dear old Hans Breitmann called them, are not quite the same as ours."

Chapter 10

THE WORDS WERE HARDLY out of his mouth before Zaidie, who still had her glasses to her eyes, and was looking down towards the great city whose glazed roofs were flashing with a thousand tints in the pale crimson sunlight, said with a little tremor in her voice:

"Look, Lenox, down there—don't you see something coming up? That little black thing. Just look how fast it's coming up; it's quite distinct already. It's a sort of flying-ship, only it has wings and, I think, masts too. Yes, I can see three masts, and there's something glittering on the tops of them. I wonder if they're coming to pay us a polite morning call, or whether they're going to treat us like trespassers in their atmosphere."

"There's no telling, but those things on top of the masts look like revolving helices," replied Redgrave, after a brief look through his telescope. "He's screwing himself up into the air. That shows that they must either have stronger and lighter machinery here than we have, or, as the astronomers have thought, this atmosphere is denser than ours and therefore easier to fly in. Then, of course, things are only half their earthly weight here.

"Well, whether it's peace or war, I suppose we may as well let them come and reconnoitre. Then we shall see what kind of creatures they are. Ah! there are a lot more of them, some coming from Brooklyn, too, as you call it. Come up into the conning-tower and I'll relieve Murgatroyd, so that he can go and look after his engines. We shall have to give these gentlemen a lesson in flying. Meanwhile, in case of accidents, we may as well make ourselves as invulnerable as possible."

A few minutes later they were in the conning-tower again, watching the approach of the Martian fleet through the thick windows of toughened glass which enabled them to look in every direction except straight down. The steel coverings had been drawn down over the glass dome of the deck-chamber, and Murgatroyd had gone down to the engine-room. Fifty feet ahead of them stretched out the long shining spur, of which ten feet were solid steel, a ram which no floating structure built by human hands could have resisted.

Redgrave was standing with his hand on the steering-wheel, looking more serious than he had done so far in the voyage. Zaidie stood beside him with a powerful binocular telescope watching, with cheeks a little paler than usual, the movements of the Martian air-ships. She counted twenty-five vessels rising round them in a wide circle.

"I don't like the idea of a whole fleet coming up," said Redgrave, as he watched them rising, and the ring narrowing round the still motionless *Astronef.* "If they only wanted to know who and what we are, or to leave their cards on us, as it were, and bid us welcome to the world, one ship could have done that just as well as a fleet. This lot coming up looks as if they wanted to get round and capture us."

"It does look like it!" said Zaidie, with her glasses fixed on the nearest of the vessels; "and now I can see they've guns, too, something like ours, and, perhaps, as you said just now. they may have explosives that we don't know anything about. Oh, Lenox, suppose they were able to smash us up with a single shot!"

"You needn't be afraid of that, dear!" he said, putting his arm round her shoulders; "Of course it's perfectly natural that they should look upon us with a certain amount of suspicion, dropping like this on them from the stars. Can you see anything like men on board them yet?"

"No, they're all closed in just as we are," she replied; "but they've got conning-towers like this, and something like windows along the sides; that's where the guns are, and the guns are moving.

They're pointing them at us. Lenox, I'm afraid they're going to shoot."

"Then we may as well spoil their aim," he said, pressing an electric button three times, and then once more after a little interval.

In obedience to the signal Murgatroyd turned on the repulsive force to half power, and the *Astronef* leapt up vertically a couple of thousand feet; then Redgrave pressed the button once and she stopped. Another signal set the propellers in motion, and as she sprang forward across the circle formed by the Martian air-ships, they looked down and saw that the place which they had just left was occupied by a thick, greenish-yellow cloud.

"Look, Lenox, what on earth is that?" exclaimed Zaidie, pointing down to it.

"What on Mars would be nearer the point, dear," he said, with what she thought a somewhat vicious laugh. "That, I'm afraid, means anything but a friendly reception for us. That cloud is one of two things—it's the smoke of the explosion of twenty or thirty shells, or else it's made of gases intended to either poison us or make us insensible, so that they can take possession of the ship. In either case I should say that the Martians are not what we should call gentlemen."

"I should think not," she said angrily. "They might at least have taken us for friends till they had proved us enemies, which they wouldn't have done. Nice sort of hospitality that, considering how far we've come, and we can't shoot back because we haven't got the ports open."

"And a very good thing too!" laughed Redgrave. "If we had had them open, and that volley had caught us unawares, the *Astronef* would probably have been full of poisonous gases by this time, and your honeymoon, dear, would have come to a somewhat untimely end. Ah, they're trying to follow us! Well, now we'll see how high they can fly."

He sent another signal to Murgatroyd, and the *Astronef*, still beating the Martian air with the fans of her propellers, and travelling forward at about fifty miles an hour, rose in a slanting direction through a dense bank of rosy-tinted clouds, which hung over the bigger of the two cities—New York, as Zaidie had named it.

When they reached the golden red sunlight above it the *Astronef* stopped her ascent, and then, with half a turn of the steering-wheel, her commander sent her sweeping round in a wide circle. A few minutes later they saw the Martian fleet rise almost simultaneously through the clouds. They seemed to hesitate a moment, and then the prow of every vessel was directed towards the swiftly moving *Astronef*.

"Well, gentlemen." said Redgrave, "you evidently don't know anything about Professor Rennick and his R.Force; and yet you ought to know that we couldn't have come through space without being able to get beyond this little atmosphere of yours. Now let us see how fast you can fly."

Another signal went down to Murgatroyd, the whirling propellers became two intersecting circles of light. The speed of the *Astronef* increased to a hundred-and-fifty miles an hour, and the Martian fleet began to drop behind and trail out into a triangle like a flock of huge birds.

"That's lovely; we're leaving them!" exclaimed Zaidie leaning forward with the glasses to her eyes and tapping the floor of the conning- tower with her toe as if she wanted to dance, "and their wings are working faster than ever. They don't seem to have any screws."

"Probably because they've solved the problem of bird's flight," said Redgrave, "They're not gaining on us, are they?"

"No, they're at about the same distance."

"Then we'll see how they can soar."

Another signal went down the tube. The *Astronef*'s propellers slowed down and stopped, and the vessel began to rise swiftly towards the Zenith, which the Sun was now approaching. The Martian fleet continued the impossible chase until the limits of the navigable atmosphere. about eight earth-miles above the surface, was reached. Here the air was evidently too rarefied for their wings to act. They came to a standstill, looking like the links of a broken chain, their occupants no doubt looking up with envious eyes upon the shining body of the *Astronef* glittering like a tiny star in the sunlight ten thousand feet above them.

"Well, gentlemen," said Redgrave after a swift glance round. "I think we have shown you that we can fly faster and soar higher than you can. Perhaps you'll be a bit more civil now. If you're not we shall have to teach you manners."

"But you're not going to fight them all dear, are you? Don't let us be the first to bring war and bloodshed with us into another world."

"Don't trouble about that, little woman, it's here already," he replied, a trifle savagely. "People don't have air-ships and guns, which fire shells or poison-bombs, or whatever they were, without knowing what war is. From what I've seen, I should say these Martians have civilised themselves out of all the emotions, and, I daresay, have fought pitilessly for the possession of the last habitable lands of the planet.

"They've preyed upon each other till only the fittest are left, and those, I suppose, were the ones who invented the air-ships and finally got possession of all that was worth having. Of course that would give them the command of the planet, land and sea. In fact, if we are able to make the personal acquaintance of the Martians, we shall probably find them a set of over-civilised savages."

"That's a rather striking paradox, isn't it, dear?" said Zaidie, slipping her hand through his arm; "but still it's not at all bad. You mean, of course, that they may have civilised themselves out of all the emotions until they're just a set of cold, calculating, scientific animals. After all they must be something of the sort, for I'm quite sure we would not have done anything like that on earth if we'd had a visitor from Mars. We shouldn't have got out cannons and shot at him before we'd even made his acquaintance.

"Now, if he, or they, had dropped in America as we were going down there, we should have received them with deputations, given them banquets, which they might not have been able to eat, and speeches, which they would not understand, and photographed them, and filled the newspapers with everything that we could imagine about them, and then put them in a palace car and hustled them round the country for everybody to look at."

"And meanwhile," laughed Redgrave. "some of your smart engineers, I suppose, would have gone over the vessel they had come in, found out how she was worked, and taken out a dozen patents for her machinery."

"Very likely," replied Zaidie, with a saucy little toss of her chin; "and why not? We like to learn things down there—and anyhow that would be much more really civilised than shooting at them."

While this little conversation was going on, the Asfronef was dropping rapidly into the midst of the Martian fleet, which had again arranged itself in a circle. Zaidie soon made out through her glasses that the guns were pointed upwards.

"Oh, that's your little game, is it!" said Redgrave, when she told him of this. "Well, if you want a fight, you can have it."

As he said this, his jaws came together, and Zaidie saw a look in his eyes that she had never seen there before. He signalled rapidly two or three times to Murgatroyd. The propellers began to whirl at their utmost speed, and the *Astronef*, making a spiral downward course, swooped down on to the Martian fleet with terrific velocity. Her last curve coincided almost exactly with the circle occupied by the ships. Half-a-dozen spouts of greenish flame came from the nearest vessel, and for a moment the *Astronef* was enveloped in a yellow mist.

"Evidently they don't know that we are air-tight, and they don't use shot or shell. They've got past that. Their projectiles kill by poison or suffocation. I daresay a volley like that would kill a regiment. Now I'll give that fellow a lesson which he won't live to remember."

They swept through the poison-mist. Redgrave swung the wheel round. The *Astronef* dropped to the level of the ring of Martian vessels, which had now got up speed again. Her steel ram was directed straight at the vessel which had fired the last shot. Propelled at a speed of nearly two hundred miles an hour, it took the strange-winged craft amidships. As the shock came, Redgrave put his arm round Zaidie's waist and held her close to him, otherwise she would have been flung against the forward wall of the conning-tower.

The Martian vessel stopped and bent up. They saw human figures more than half as large again as men inside her staring at them through the windows in the sides. There were others at the breaches of the guns in the act of turning the muzzles on the

Astronef; but this was only a momentary glimpse, for in a second the *Astronef*'s spur had pierced her, the Martian air-ship broke in twain, and her two halves plunged downwards through the rosy clouds.

"Keep her at full speed, Andrew." said Redgrave down the speaking-tube, "and stand by to jump if we want to."

"All ready, my lord!" came back up the tube.

The old Yorkshireman during the last few minutes had undergone a transformation which he himself hardly understood. He recognised that there was a fight going on, that it was a case of' burn, sink and destroy, "and the thousand-year-old savage awoke in him just, as a matter of fact, it had done in his lordship.

"They can pick up the pieces down there, what there is left of them," said Redgrave, still holding Zaidie tight to his side with one hand and working the wheel with the other. "and now we'll teach them another lesson."

"What are you going to do, dear?" she said, looking up at him with somewhat frightened eyes.

"You'll see in a moment," he said, between his shut teeth. "I don't care whether these Martians are degenerate human beings or only animals; but from my point of view the reception that they have given us justifies any kind of retaliation. If we'd had a single port hole open during the first volley you and I would have been dead by this time, and I'm not going to stand anything like that without reprisals. They've declared war on us, and killing in war isn't murder."

"Well, no, I suppose not," she said; "but it's the first fight I've been in, and I don't like it. Still, they did receive us pretty meanly, didn't they?"

"Meanly? If there was anything like a code of interplanetary morals, one might call it absolutely caddish. I don't believe even Stead himself could stand that—unless, of course, he wasn't here."

He sent another message to Murgatroyd. The *Astronef* sprang a thousand feet towards the zenith; another signal, and she stopped exactly over the biggest of the Martian air-ships; another, and she dropped on to it like a stone and smashed it to fragments. Then she stopped and mounted again above the broken circle of the fleet, while the pieces of the air-ship and what was left of her crew plunged downwards through the crimson clouds in a fall of nearly thirty thousand feet.

Within the next few moments the rest of the Martian fleet had followed it, sinking rapidly down through the clouds and scattering in all directions.

"They seem to have had enough of it," laughed Redgrave, as the *Astronef*, in obedience to another signal, began to drop towards the surface of Mars. "Now we'll go down and see if they're in a more reasonable frame of mind. At any rate we've won our first scrimmage, dear."

"But it was rather brutal, Lenox, wasn't it?"

"When you are dealing with brutes, little woman, it is sometimes necessary to be brutal."

"And you look a wee bit brutal now," she replied, looking up at him with something like a look of fear in her eyes. "I suppose that is because you have just killed somebody—or somethings—whichever they are."

"Do I, really?"

The hard-set jaw relaxed and his lips melted into a smile under his moustache, and he bent down and kissed her.

"Well, what do you suppose I should have thought of them if you had had a whiff of that poison?"

"Yes, dear," she whispered in between the kisses, "I see now."

CHAPTER 11

THE *ASTRONEF* DROPPED SWIFTLY down through the crimson-tinged clouds, and a few minutes later they saw that the fleet had scattered in units in all directions, apparently with the intention of getting as far as possible out of reach of that terrible ram. Only one of them, the largest, which carried what looked like a flag of woven gold at the top of its centre mast, remained in sight after a few minutes. It was almost immediately below them when they had passed through the clouds, and they could see it sinking straight down towards the centre of what appeared to be the principal square of the bigger of the two cities which Zaidie had named New York and Brooklyn.

"That fellow has gone to report, evidently," said Redgrave. "We'll follow him just to see what he's up to, but I don't think we'd better open the ports even then. There's no telling when they might give us a whiff of that poison-mist, or whatever it is."

"But how are you going to talk to them, then, if they can talk?—I mean, if they know any language that we do?"

"They're something like men, and so I suppose they understand the language of signs, at any rate. Still, if you don't fancy it, we'll go somewhere else."

"No thanks," she said. "That's not my father's daughter. I haven't come a hundred million miles from home to go away before the first act's finished. We'll go down to see if we can make them understand."

By this time the *Astronef* was hanging suspended over an enormous square about half the size of Hyde Park. It was laid out just as a terrestrial park would be in grassland, flower beds, and avenues, and patches of trees, only the grass was a reddish yellow, the leaves of the trees were like those of a beech in autumn, and the flowers were nearly all a deep violet, or a bright emerald green.

As they descended they saw that the square, or Central Park, as Zaidie at once christened it, was flanked by enormous blocks of buildings, palaces built of a dazzlingly white stone, and topped by domed roofs and lofty cupolas of glass.

"Isn't that just lovely!" she said, swinging her binoculars in every direction. "Talk about your Park Lane and the houses round Central Park; why, it's the Chicago Exposition, and the Paris one, and your Crystal Palace, multiplied by about ten thousand, and all spread out just round this one place. If we don't find these people nice, I guess we'd better go back and build a fleet like this, and come and take it."

"There spoke the new American imperialism" laughed Redgrave. "Well, we'll go and see what they're like first, shall we?"

The *Astronef* dropped a little more slowly than the air-ship had done, and remained suspended a hundred feet or so above her after she had reached the ground. Swarms of human figures, but of more than human stature, clad in tunics and trousers or knickerbockers, came out of the glass-domed palaces from all sides into the park. They were nearly all of the same stature and there appeared to be no difference whatever between the sexes. Their dress was absolutely plain; there was no attempt at ornament or decoration of any kind.

"If there are any of the Martian women among those people," said her ladyship, "they've taken to rationals and they've grown about as big as the men.

That's exactly what's happening on earth, you know, dear. I don't mean about the rationals, but the women growing up, especially in America. I come of a pretty long family—but look!"

"Well, I only come to your ear," she said.

"And our descendants of ten thousand years hence—"

"Oh, don't bother about them!" she said. "Look; there's someone who seems to want to communicate with us. Why, they're all bald! They haven't got a hair among them—and what a size their heads are!"

"That's brains—too much brains, in fact! These people have lived too long. I daresay they've ceased to be animals—civilised themselves out of everything in the way of passions and emotions, and are just purely intellectual beings, with as much human nature about them as Russian diplomacy or those things we saw at the bottom of Newton crater. I don't like the look of them."

The orderly swarms of figures, which were rapidly filling the park, divided as he was speaking, making a broad lane from one of its entrances to where the *Astronef* was hanging above the air-ship. A light four-wheeled vehicle, whose framework and wheels glittered like burnished gold, sped towards them, driven by some invisible agency.

Its only occupant was a huge man, dressed in the universal costume, saving only a scarlet sash in place of the cord-girdle which the others wore round their waists. The vehicle stopped near the air-ship, over which the *Astronef* was hanging, and, as the figure dismounted, a door opened in the side of the vessel and three other figures, similar both in stature and attire, came out and entered into conversation with him.

"The Admiral of the Fleet is evidently making his report," said Redgrave. "Meanwhile, the crowd seems to be taking a considerable amount of interest in us."

"And very naturally, too!" replied Zaidie. "Don't you think we might go down now and see if we can make ourselves understood in any way? You can have the guns ready in case of accidents, but I don't think they'll try and hurt us now. Look, the gentleman with the red sash is making signs."

"I think we can go down now all right," replied Redgrave, "because it's quite certain they can't use the poison guns on us without killing themselves as well. Still, we may as well have our own ready. Andrew, get that port Maxim ready. I hope we shan't want it, but we may. I don't quite like the look of these people."

"They're very ugly, aren't they?" said Zaidie; "and really you can't tell which are men and which are women. I suppose they've civilised themselves out of everything that's nice, and are just

Stanley L Wood

scientific and utilitarian and everything that's horrid."

"I shouldn't wonder. They look to me as if they've just got common sense, as we call it, and hadn't any other sense; but, at any rate, if they don't behave themselves, we shall be able to teach them manners of a sort, though we may possibly have done that to some extent already."

As he said this Redgrave went into the conning-tower, and the *Astronef* moved from above the air-ship, and dropped gently into the crimson grass about a hundred feet from her. Then the ports were opened, the guns, which Murgatroyd had loaded, were swung into position, and they armed themselves with a brace of revolvers each, in case of accident.

"What delicious air this is!" said her ladyship, as the ports were opened, and she took her first breath of the Martian atmosphere. "It's ever so much nicer than ours; it's just like breathing champagne."

Redgrave looked at her with an admiration which was tempered by a sudden apprehension. Even in his eyes she had never seemed so lovely before. Her cheeks were glowing and her eyes were gleaming with a brightness that was almost feverish, and he was himself sensible of a strange feeling of exultation, both mental and physical, as his lungs filled with the Martian air.

"Oxygen," he said shortly, "and too much of it! Or, I shouldn't wonder if it was something like nitrous-oxide—you know, laughing gas."

"Don't!" she laughed, "it may be very nice to breath. but it reminds one of other things which aren't a bit nice. Still, if it is anything of that sort it might account for these people having lived so fast. I know I feel just now as if I were living at the rate of thirty-six hours a day and so, I suppose, the fewer hours we stop here the better."

"Exactly!' said Redgrave, with another glance of apprehension at her. Now, there's his Royal Highness, or whatever he is, coming. How are we going to talk to him? Are you all ready, Andrew?"

"Yes, my lord, all ready" replied the old Yorkshireman, dropping his huge, hairy hand on the breach of the Maxim.

"Very well, then, shoot the moment you see them doing anything suspicious, and don't let anyone except his Royal Highness come nearer than a hundred yards."

As he said this Redgrave went to the door, from which the gangway steps had been lowered, and, in reply to a singularly expressive gesture from the huge Martian, who seemed to stand nearly nine feet high, he beckoned to him to come up on to the deck.

As he mounted the steps the crowd closed round the *Astronef* and the Martian air-ship; but, as though in obedience to orders which had already been given, they kept at a respectful distance of a little over a hundred yards away from the strange vessel, which had wrought such havoc with their fleet. When the Martian reached the deck, Redgrave held out his hand and the giant recoiled, as a man on earth might have done if, instead of the open palm, he had seen a clenched hand gripping a knife.

"Take care, Lenox," exclaimed Zaidie, taking a couple of steps towards him, with her right hand on the butt of one of her revolvers. The movement brought her close to the open door, and in full view of the crowd outside.

If a seraph had come on earth and presented itself thus before a throng of human beings, there might have happened some such miracle as was wrought when the swarm of Martians beheld the strange beauty of this radiant daughter of the earth.

As it seemed to the space-voyagers, when they discussed it afterwards, ages of purely utilitarian civilisation had brought all conditions of Martian life up—or down—to the same level. There was no apparent difference between the males and females in stature; their faces were all the same, with features of mathematical regularity, pale skin, bloodless cheeks, and an expression, if such it could be called, utterly devoid of emotion.

But still these creatures were human, or at least their forefathers had been. Hearts beat in their breasts, blood of a sort still flowed through their veins, and so the magic of this marvellous vision instantly awoke the long-slumbering elementary instincts of a byegone age. A low murmur ran through the vast throng, a murmur half-human, half-brutish, which swiftly rose to a hoarse screaming roar.

"Look out, my lord! Quick! Shut the door, they're coming! It's her ladyship they want; she must look like an angel from Heaven to them. Shall I fire?"

"Yes," said Redgrave, gripping the lever, and bringing the door down. "Zaidie, if this fellow moves, put a bullet through him. I'm going to talk to that air-ship before he gets his poison guns to work."

As the last word left his lips, Murgatroyd put his thumb on the spring on the Maxim. A roar such as Martian ears had never heard before resounded through the vast square, and was flung back with a thousand echoes from the walls of the huge palaces on every side. A stream of smoke and flame poured out of the little port-hole, and then the onward-swarming throng seemed to stop, and the front ranks of it began to sink down silently in long rows.

Then through the roaring rattle of the Maxim sounded the deep, sharp bang of Redgrave's gun, as he sent twenty pounds' weight of Rennickite, as he had christened it, into the Martian air-ship. There was the roar of an explosion which shook the air for miles around. A blaze of greenish flame and a huge cloud of steamy smoke showed that the projectile had done its work, and, when the smoke drifted away, the spot on which the air-ship had lain

was only a deep, red, jagged gash in the ground. There was not even a fragment of the ship to be seen.

This done, Redgrave went and turned the starboard Maxim on to another swarm which was approaching the *Astronef* from that side. When he had got the range, he swung the gun slowly from side to side. The moving throng stopped, as the other one had done, and sank down to the red grass, now dyed with a deeper red.

Meanwhile, Zaidie had been holding the Martian at something more than arm's length with her revolver. He seemed to understand perfectly that, if she pulled the trigger, the revolver would do something like what the Maxims had done. He appeared to take no notice whatever either of the destruction of the airship or of the slaughter that was going on around the *Astronef.* His big pale blue eyes were fixed upon her face. They seemed to be devouring a loveliness such as they had never seen before. A dim, pinky flush stole for the first time into his waxy cheeks, and something like a light of human passion came into his eyes.

Then, to the utter astonishment of both Redgrave and Zaidie, he said slowly and deliberately, and with only just enough tinge of emotion in his voice to make Redgrave want to shoot him:

"Beautiful. Perfect. More perfect than ours. I want it. Give Palace and Garden of Eternal Summer for it. Two thousand work-slaves and fifty—"

"And I'll see you damned first, sir, whoever you are!" said Redgrave, clapping his hand on to the butt of the revolver, and forgetting for the moment that he was speaking in another world than his own. "What the devil do you mean, sir, by insulting my wife—?"

"Insulting. Wife. What is that? We have no words like those."

"But you speak English," exclaimed Zaidie, going a little nearer to him, but still keeping the muzzle of her revolver pointing up to his hairless head. "No, Lenox, don't be afraid about me, and don't get angry. Can't you see that this person hasn't got any temper? I suppose it was civilised out of his ancestors ages ago. He doesn't know what a wife or an insult is. He just looks upon me as a desirable piece of property to be bought, and I daresay he offered you a very handsome price. Now, don't look so savage, because you know bargains like that have been made even on our dear old virtuous Mother Earth. For instance, if you hadn't met us in the middle of the Atlantic—"

"That'll do, Zaidie," Redgrave interrupted almost roughly. "That's not exactly the question, but I see what you mean, and it was a bit silly of me to get angry."

"Silly? Angry? What do those words mean?" said the Martian in his slow, passionless, mechanical voice "Who are you? Whence come you?"

"I'll answer the last part first," said Redgrave.

"We come from the earth, the planet which you see after sunset and before sunrise."

"Yes, the Silver Star," said the Martian without any note of wonder or surprise in his voice. "Are all the dwellers there like the gods and angels our children read about in the old legends?"

"Gods and angels!" laughed Zaidie. "There, Lenox, there's a compliment for you. I really think we ought to be as civil to his Royal Highness after that as possible." Then she went on, addressing the Martian, "No, we are not all gods and angels on earth. There are no gods and very few angels. In fact there are none except those which exist in the fancy of certain prejudiced persons. But that doesn't matter, at least not just now," she continued with American directness. "What we want to know just now is, why you speak English, and what sort of a world this Mars is?"

The Martian evidently only understood the most direct essentials of her speech. He saw that she asked two questions, and he answered them.

"Speak English?" he replied, with a little shake of his huge head. "We know not English, but there is no other speech. There is only ours. Cycles ago there were other speeches here, but those who spoke them were killed. It was inconvenient. One speech for a world is best."

"I see what he means," said Redgrave, looking towards Zaidie. "The Martian people have developed along practically the same lines as we are doing, but they have done it faster and got a long way ahead of us. We are finding out that the speech we call English is the shortest and most convenient. The Martians found it out long ago and killed everybody who spoke anything else. After all, what we call speech is only the translation of thoughts into sounds. These people have been thinking for ages with the same sort of brains as ours, and they've translated their thoughts into the same sounds. What we call English they, I daresay, call Martian, and that's all there is in it that I can see."

"Of course," laughed Zaidie. "Wonderful until you know how, eh? Like most things. Still I must say that our friend here speaks English something like a phonograph, and if he'll excuse me saying so, which of course he will, he doesn't seem to have much more human nature about him."

"I'm not quite so sure on that point," said Redgrave, "but—"

"Oh, never mind about that now!" she interrupted, and then, turning towards the Martian, who had been listening intently as though he was trying to make sense out of what they had been saying, she went on speaking slowly and very plainly-

"Tell me, sir, if you please, do you know what 'angry' means? Are you not angry with us for destroying your air-ships up there in the clouds, and the one that came down, and for shooting all those people of yours?"

The Martian looked at her with a little light in his big blue eyes, and two faint little spots of red just under them, and said: "Anger! Yes, I remember, that is what we called brain-heat. Our teachers found it to be madness and it was abolished. It was not convenient. The air-ships were not convenient to you, so you abolished them. The folk, too, that you abolished with those things," pointing to the guns, "they were not convenient. If you hadn't done that they would have abolished you. There is no more to say."

"What brutes," said Zaidie, turning away from him, her head thrown back and her lips curling in unutterable disgust. "Well, if these people have civilised themselves along the same lines that we are doing, thinking the same things and speaking something like the same speech, thank God we shall be dead before our civilisation reaches a stage like this. That's not a man. It's only a machine of

flesh and bone and nerves, and I suppose it has blood of some sort.

A beautiful woman always looks most beautiful when she is just a little angry. Redgrave had never seen Zaidie look quite so lovely as she did just then. The Martian, whose ancestors had for generations forgotten what human emotion was like, only saw in her anger a miracle which made her a thousand times more beautiful than before, and as he looked upon her glowing cheeks and gleaming eyes some instinct insensibly transmitted through many generations awoke to sudden life in some unused corner of his brain.

His pale clear eyes lit up with something like a glow of human passion. The pink spots under his eyes spread downwards over his cheeks. Some half-articulate sounds came from between his thin lips. Then they were drawn back and showed his smooth, toothless gums. He took a couple of long, swift strides towards her, and then bent forward, towering over her with long, outstretched arms, huge, hideous, and half-human. Zaidie sprang backwards as he came towards her, her right hand went up, and, just as Redgrave levelled his revolver, and Murgatroyd, true to the old Berserk instinct, took a rifle by the barrel and swung the stock above his head, Zaidie pulled her trigger. The bullet cut a clean hole through the smooth, hairless skull of the Martian. A dark, red spot came just between his eyes, his huge frame shrank together and collapsed in a heap on the deck.

"Oh, I've killed him! God forgive me, killed a man!" she whispered, as her hand fell to her side, and the revolver dropped from her fingers. "But, Lenox, do you really think it was a man?"

"That thing a man!" he replied between his clenched teeth. "He wanted you, and spoke English of a sort, so there was something human about him, but anyhow he's better dead. Here, Andrew, open that door again and help me to heave this thing overboard. Then I think we'd better be off before we have the rest of the fleet with their poison guns round us. Zaidie, I think you'd better go to your room for the present. Take a nip of cognac and then lie down, and mind you keep the door tight shut. There's no telling what these animals might do if they had a chance, and just now it's my business and Andrew's to see that they don't."

Though she would much rather have remained on deck to see anything more that might happen, she saw that he was really in earnest, and so like a wise wife who commands by obeying, she obeyed, and went below.

Then the dead body of the Martian was tumbled out of the side door. The windows through which the guns had been fired were hermetically closed, and a few minutes later the *Astronef* vanished from the surface of Mars, to remain a memory and a marvel to the dwindling generations of the worn-out world which is as this may be in the far-off days that are to come.

CHAPTER 12

"HOW VERY DIFFERENT Venus looks now to what it does from the earth," said Zaidie, a couple of mornings later, by earth-time, as she took her eye away from the telescope through which she had been examining an enormous golden crescent which spanned the dark vault of space ahead of and slightly below the *Astronef*.

"Yes," replied Redgrave, "she looks—"

"How do you know that she is a she?" said Zaidie, getting up and laying a hand on his shoulder as he sat at his own telescope. "Of course I know what you mean, that according to our own ideas on Earth, it is the planet or the world which has been supposed for ages to, as it were, shine on the lovers of earth with the light reflected from the—the—well, I suppose you know what I mean."

"Seeing that you are the most perfect terrestrial incarnation of the said goddess that I have seen yet," he replied, slipping his arm round her waist and pulling her down onto his knees, "I don't think that this is quite the view you ought to take. Surely if Venus ever had a daughter—"

"Oh, nonsense! After we've travelled all these millions of miles together do you really expect me to believe stuff like that?"

"My dear girl-graduate," he said, tightening his grip round her waist a little, "you know perfectly well that if we had travelled beyond the limits of the Solar System, if we had outsailed old Halley's Comet itself, and dived into the uttermost depths of Space outside the Milky Way, you and I would still be a man and a woman, and, being, as may be presumed, more or less in love with each other—"

"Less indeed!" said Zaidie; "you're speaking for yourself, I hope."

And then when she had partially disengaged herself and sat up straight, she said between her laughs—

"Really, Lenox, you're quite absurd for a person who has been married as long as you have, I don't mean in time, but in space. Was it a thousand years or a couple of hundred million miles ago that we were married? Really I am getting my ideas of time and space quite mixed up.

"But never mind that! What I was going to say is that, according to all the authorities which your girl-graduate has been reading since we left Mars, Venus —oh, doesn't she look just gorgeous, and our old friend the Sun behind there blazing out of darkness like one of the furnaces at Pittsburg—I beg your pardon, Lenox, I'm afraid I'm getting quite provincial. I suppose we're considerably more than a hundred million miles away?"

"Yes, dear; we're about a hundred and fifty millions, and at that distance, if you'll excuse me saying so, even the United States would seem almost like a province, wouldn't they?"

"Well, yes; that's just where distance doesn't lend enchantment to the view, I suppose."

"But what was it you were going to say before that—"

"The interlude, eh? Well, before the interlude you were accusing me of being a graduate as well as a girl. Of course I can't help that, but what I was going to say was—"

"If you are going to talk science, dear, perhaps we'd better sit on different chairs. I may have been married for a hundred and fifty million miles, but the honeymoon isn't half way through yet, you know."

Then there was another interlude of a few seconds' duration. When Zaidie was seated beside her own telescope again, she said, after another glance at the splendid crescent which, as the *Astronef* approached at a speed of over forty miles a second, increased in size and distinctness every moment:

"What I mean is this. All the authorities are agreed that on Venus, her axis of revolution bang so very much inclined to the plane of her orbit, the seasons are so severe that half the year its temperate zone and its tropics have a summer about twice as hot as ours tropics and the other half they have a winter twice as cold as our coldest. I'm afraid, after all, we shall find the Love-Star a world of salamanders and seals; things that can live in a furnace and bask on an iceberg; and when we get back home it will be our painful duty, as the first explorers of the fields of space, to dispel another dearly-cherished popular delusion."

"I'm not so very sure about that," said Lenox, glancing from the rapidly growing crescent, to the sweet smiling face beside him. "Don't you see something very different there to what we saw either on the Moon or Mars? Now just go back to your telescope and let us take an observation."

"Well," said Zaidie, rising, "as our trip is partly, at least, in the interest of science, I will." and then, when she had got her own telescope into focus again—for the distance between the *Astronef* and the new world they were about to visit was rapidly lessening—she took a long look through it, and said:

"Yes, I think I see what you mean. The outer edge of the crescent is bright, but it gets greyer and dimmer towards the inside of the curve. Of course Venus has an atmosphere. So had Mars; but this must be very dense. There's a sort of halo all round it. Just fancy that splendid thing being the little black spot we saw going across the face of the Sun a few days ago! It makes one feel rather small, doesn't it?"

"That is one of the things which a woman says when she doesn't want to be answered; but, apart from that, you were saying—"

"What a very unpleasant person you can be when you like! I was going to say that on the Moon we saw nothing but black and white, light and darkness. There was no atmosphere, except in those awful places I don't want to think about. Then, as we got near Mars, we saw a pinky atmosphere, but not very dense; but this, you see, is a sort of pearl-grey white shading from silver to black. But look—what are those tiny bright spots? There are hundreds of them."

"Do you remember as we were leaving the earth, how bright the mountain ranges looked; how plainly we could see the Rockies and the Andes?"

"Oh, yes, I see; they're mountains; thirty-seven miles high some of them, they say; and the rest of the silver-grey will be clouds, I suppose. Fancy living under clouds like those."

"Only another case of the adaptation of life to natural conditions, I expect. When we get there, I daresay we shall find that these clouds are just what make it possible for the inhabitants of Venus to stand the extremes of heat and cold. Given elevations, three or four times as high as the Himalayas, it would be quite possible for them to choose their temperature by shifting their altitude.

"But I think it's about time to drop theory and see to the practice," he continued, getting up from his chair and going to the signal board to the conning-tower. "Whatever the planet Venus may be like, we don't want to charge it at the rate of sixty miles a second. That's about the speed now, considering how fast she's travelling towards us."

"And considering that, whether it is a nice world or not, it's nearly as big as the earth, I guess we should get rather the worst of the charge," laughed Zaidie, as she went back to her telescope.

Redgrave sent a signal down to Murgatroyd to reverse engines, as it were, or, in other words, to direct the "R. Force" against the planet, from which they were now only a couple of hundred thousand miles distant. The next moment the sun and stars seemed to halt in their courses. The great golden-grey crescent which had been increasing in size every moment, appeared to remain stationary, and then, when he was satisfied that the engines were developing the Force properly, he sent another signal down, and the *Astronef* began to descend.

The half-disc of Venus seemed to fall below them, and in a few minutes they could see it from the upper deck spreading out like a huge semi-circular plain of light ahead and on both sides of them. The *Astronef* was falling upon it at the rate of about a thousand miles a minute towards the centre of the half crescent, and every moment the brilliant spots above the cloud-surface grew in size and brightness.

"I believe the theory about the enormous height of the

mountains of Venus must be correct after all," said Redgrave, tearing himself with an evident wrench away from his telescope. "Those white patches can't be anything else but the summits of snow-capped mountains. You know how brilliantly white a snow-peak looks on earth against the whitest of clouds."

"Oh, yes," said Zaidie, "I've often seen that in the Rockies. But it's lunch time, and I must go down and see how my things in the kitchen are getting on. I suppose you'll try and land somewhere where it's morning, so that we can have a good day before us. Really, it's very convenient to be able to make your own morning or night as you like, isn't it? I hope it won't make us too conceited when we get back, being able to choose our mornings and our evenings; in fact, our sunrises and sunsets on any world we like to visit in a casual way like this."

"Well," laughed Redgrave, as she moved away towards the companion stairs, "after all, if you find the United States, or even the planet Terra, too small for you, we've always got the fields of Space open to us. We might take a trip across the Zodiac or down the Milky Way."

"And meanwhile," she replied, stopping at the top of the stairs and looking round, "I'll go down and get lunch. You and I may be king and queen of the realms of Space, and all that sort of thing, but we've got to eat and drink, after all."

"And that reminds me," said Redgrave, getting up and following her, "we must celebrate our arrival on a new world as usual. I'll go down and get out the wine. I shouldn't be surprised if we found the people of the Love-World living on nectar and ambrosia, and as fizz is our nearest approach to nectar—"

"I suppose," said Zaidie, as she gathered up her skirts and stepped daintily down the companion stairs, "if you find anything human or at least human enough to eat and drink, you'll have a party and give them champagne. I wonder what those wretches on Mars would have thought of it if we'd only made friends with them?"

Lunch on board the *Astronef* was about the pleasantest meal of the day. Of course there was neither day nor night, in the ordinary sense of the word, except as the hours were measured off by the chronometers. Whichever side or end of the vessel received the direct rays of the sun, was bathed in blazing heat and dazzling light. Elsewhere there was black darkness, and the more than icy cold of space; but lunch was a convenient division of the waking hours, which began with a stroll on the upper deck and a view of the ever-varying splendours about them, and ended after dinner in the same place with coffee and cigarettes and speculations as to the next day's happenings.

This lunch hour passed even more pleasantly and rapidly than others had done, for the discussion as to the possibilities of Venus was continued in a quite delightful mixture of scientific disquisition and that converse which is common to most human beings on their honeymoon.

As there was nothing more to be done or seen for an hour or two, the afternoon was spent in a pleasant siesta in the luxurious deck-saloon; because evening to them would be morning on that portion of Venus to which they were directing their course, and, as Zaidie said, when she subsided into her hammock:

It would be breakfast-time before they could get dinner.

As the *Astronef* fell with ever-increasing velocity towards the cloud-covered surface of Venus, the remainder of her disc, lit up by the radiance of her sister-worlds, Mercury, Mars, and the Earth, and also by the pale radiance of an enormous comet, which had suddenly shot into view from behind its southern limb, became more or less visible.

Towards six o'clock it became necessary to exert the full strength of her engines to check the velocity of her fall. By eight she had entered the atmosphere of Venus, and was dropping slowly towards a vast sea of sunlit cloud, out of which, on all sides, towered thousands of snow-clad peaks, rounded summits, and widespread stretches of upland above which the clouds swept and surged like the silent billows of some vast ocean in Ghostland.

"I thought so!" said Redgrave, when the propellers had begun to revolve and Murgatroyd had taken his place in the conning-tower. "A very dense atmosphere loaded with clouds. There's the sun just rising, so your ladyship's wishes are duly obeyed."

"And doesn't it seem nice and homelike to see him rising through an atmosphere above the clouds again? It doesn't look a bit like the same sort of dear old sun just blazing like a red-hot moon among a lot of white hot stars and planets. Look, aren't those peaks lovely, and that cloud-sea?—Why, for all the world we might be in a balloon above the Rockies or the Alps. And see," she continued, pointing to one of the thermometers fixed outside the glass dome which covered the upper deck, "it's only sixty-five even here. I wonder if we can breathe this air, and oh, I do wonder what we shall see on the other side of those clouds."

"You shall have both questions answered in a few minutes," replied Redgrave, going towards the conning-tower. "To begin with, I think we'll land on that big snow-dome yonder, and do a little exploring. Where there are snow and clouds there is moisture, and where there is moisture a man ought to be able to breathe."

The *Astronef*, still falling, but now easily under the command of the helmsman, shot forwards and downwards towards a vast dome of snow which, rising some two thousand feet above the cloud-sea, shone with dazzling brilliance in the light of the rising Sun. She landed just above the edge of the clouds. Meanwhile they had put on their breathing-suits, and Redgrave had seen that the air chamber through which they had to pass from their own little world into the new ones that they visited was in working order. When the outer door was opened and the ladder lowered he stood aside, as he had done on the moon, and Zaidie's was the first human foot which made an imprint on the virgin snows of Venus.

The first thing Lenox did was to raise the visor of his helmet and taste the air of the new world. It was cool, and fresh, and sweet, and the first draught of it sent the blood tingling and dancing through his veins. Perfect as the arrangements of the *Astronef* were in this respect, the air of Venus tasted like clear running spring water would have done to a man who had been drinking filtered water for several days. He threw the visor right up and motioned to Zaidie to do the same. She obeyed, and, after drawing a long breath, she said:

"That's glorious! It's like wine after water, and rather stagnant water too. But what a world, snow-peaks and cloud-sea, islands of

ice and snow in an ocean of mist! Just look at them! Did you ever see anything so lovely and unearthly in your life? I wonder how high this mountain is, and what there is on the other side of the clouds. Isn't the air delicious! Not a bit too cold after all—but, still, I think we may as well go back and put on something more becoming. I shouldn't quite like the ladies of Venus to see me dressed like a diver."

"Come along then," laughed Lenox, as he turned back towards the vessel. "That's just like a woman. You're about a hundred and fifty million miles away from Broadway or Regent Street. You are standing on the top of a snow mountain above the clouds of Venus, and the moment that you find the air is fit to breathe you begin thinking about dress. How do you know that the inhabitants of Venus, if there are any, dress at all?"

"What nonsense! Of course they do—at least, if they are anything like us."

As soon as they got back on board the *Astronef* and had taken their breathing-dresses off, Redgrave and the old engineer, who appeared to take no visible interest in their new surroundings, lay many thousands of feet below.

"What a lovely world!" said Zaidie, as she at last found her voice after what was almost a stupor of speechless wonder and admiration. "And the light! Did you ever see anything like it? It's neither moonlight nor sunlight. See, there are no shadows down there, it's just all lovely silvery twilight. Lenox, if Venus is as nice as she looks from here I don't think I shall want to go back. It reminds me of Tennyson's Lotus Eaters, 'The land where it is always afternoon.'

"I think you are right after all. We are thirty million miles nearer to the sun than we were on the earth, and the light and heat have to filter through those clouds. They are not at all like earth-clouds from this side. It's the other way about. The silver lining is on this side. Look, there isn't a black or a brown one, or even a grey one, within sight. They are just like a thin mist, lighted by millions of electric lamps. It's a delicious world, and if it isn't inhabited by angels it ought to be."

Chapter 13

WHILE THEY WERE TALKING, the *Astronef* was sweeping swiftly down towards the surface of Venus, through scenery of whose almost inconceivable magnificence no human words could convey any adequate idea. Underneath the cloud-veil the air was absolutely clear and transparent; clearer, indeed, than terrestrial air at the highest elevations, and, moreover, it seemed to be endowed with a strange luminous quality, which made objects, no matter how distant, stand out with almost startling distinctness.

The rivers and lakes and seas which spread out beneath them, seemed never to have been ruffled by the blast of a storm or breath of wind, and their surfaces shone with a soft silvery light, which seemed to come from below rather than from above.

"If this isn't heaven it must be the half-way house," said Redgrave, with what was, perhaps, under the circumstances, a pardonable irreverence. "Still, after all, we don't know what the inhabitants may be like, so I think we'd better close the doors, and drop on the top of that mountain spur running out between the two rivers into the bay. Do you notice how curious the water looks after the earth-seas; bright silver, instead of blue and green?"

"Oh, it's just lovely," said Zaidie. "Let's go down and have a walk. There's nothing to be afraid of. You'll never make me believe that a world like this can be inhabited by anything dangerous.

"Perhaps, but we mustn't forget what happened on Mars, Madonna Mia. still, there's one thing, we haven't been tackled by any aerial fleets yet."

"I don't think the people here want air-ships. They can fly themselves. Look! there are a lot of them coming to meet us. That was a rather wicked remark of yours about the half-way house to Heaven; but those certainly look something like angels.

As Zaidie said this, after a somewhat lengthy pause, during which the *Astronef* had descended to within a few hundred feet of the mountain-spur, she handed a pair of field-glasses to her husband, and pointed downward towards an island which lay a couple of miles or so off the end of the spur.

Redgrave put the glasses to his eyes, and took a long look through them. Moving them slowly up and down, and from side to side, he saw hundreds of winged figures rising from the island and soaring towards them.

"You were right, dear," he said, without taking the glass from his eyes, "and so was I. If those aren't angels, they're certainly something like men, and, I suppose, women too who can fly. We may as well stop here and wait for them. I wonder what sort of an animal they take the *Astronef* for."

He sent a message down the tube to Murgatroyd, and gave a turn and a half to the steering wheel. The propellers slowed down and the *Astronef* dropped with a hardly perceptible shock in the midst of a little plateau covered with a thick, soft moss of a pale yellowish green, and fringed by a belt of trees which seemed to be over three hundred feet high, and whose foliage was a deep golden bronze.

They had scarcely landed before the flying figures reappeared over the tree-tops and swept downwards in long spiral curves towards the *Astronef*.

"If they're not angels, they're very like them," said Zaidie, putting down her glasses.

"There's one thing," replied her husband; "they fly a lot better than the old masters' angels or Dore's could have done, because they have tails—or at least something that seems to serve the same purpose, and yet they haven't got feathers."

"Yes, they have, at least round the edges of their wings or whatever they are, and they've got clothes, too, silk tunics or something of that sort—and there are men and women."

"You're quite right. Those fringes down their legs are feathers, and that's how they fly. They seem to have four arms."

The flying figures which came hovering near to the *Astronef*, without evincing any apparent sign of fear, were certainly the strangest that human eyes had looked upon. In some respects they had a sufficient resemblance to human form for them to be taken for winged men and women, while in another they bore a decided resemblance to birds. Their bodies and limbs were almost human in shape, but of slenderer and lighter build; and from the shoulder-blades and muscles of the back there sprang a pair of wings arching up above their heads. Between these and the lower arms, and continued from them down the sides to the ankles, there appeared to be a flexible membrane covered with a light feathery down, pure white on the inside, but on the back a brilliant golden yellow, deepening to bronze towards the edges, round which ran a deep feathery fringe.

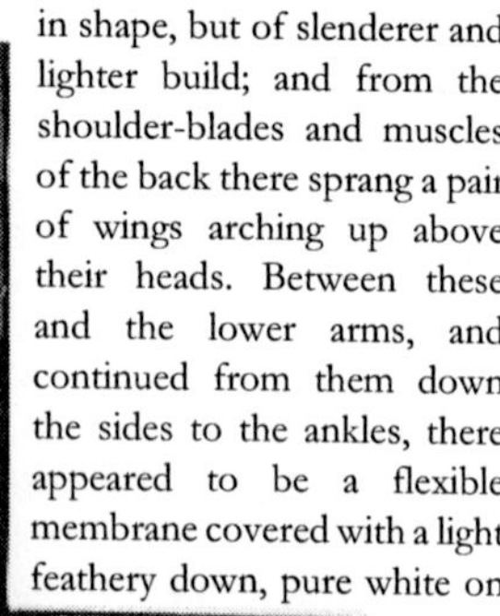

The body was covered in front and down the back between the wings with a sort of divided tunic of a light, silken-looking material, which must have been clothing, since there were many different colours all more or less of different hue among them. Below this and attached to the inner sides of the leg from the knee downward, was another membrane which reached down to the heels, and it was this which Redgrave somewhat flippantly alluded to as a tail. Its obvious purpose was to maintain the longitudinal balance when flying.

In stature these inhabitants of the Love-Star varied from about five feet six to five feet, but both the taller and the shorter of them were all of nearly the same size, from which it was easy to conclude that this difference in stature was on Venus, as well as on the Earth, one of the broad distinctions between the sexes.

They flew once or twice completely round the *Astronef* with an exquisite ease and grace which made Zaidie exclaim:

"Now, why weren't we made like that on Earth!"

To which Redgrave, after a look at the barometer, replied:

"Partly, I suppose, because we weren't built that way, and partly because we don't live in an atmosphere about two and a half times as dense as ours."

Then several of the winged figures alighted on the mossy covering of the plain and walked towards the vessel.

"Why, they walk just like us, only much more prettily!" said Zaidie. "And look what funny little faces they've got! Half bird, half human, and soft, downy feathers instead of hair. I wonder whether they talk or sing. I wish you'd open the doors again, Lenox. I'm sure they can't possibly mean us any harm; they are far too pretty for that. What lovely soft eyes they have, and what a thousand pities it is we shan't be able to understand them."

They had left the conning-tower and both his lordship and Murgatroyd were throwing open the sliding doors and, to Zaidie's considerable displeasure, getting the deck Maxims ready for action in case they should be required. As soon as the doors were open Zaidie's judgement of the inhabitants of Venus was entirely justified.

Without the slightest sign of fear, but with very evident astonishment in their round golden-yellow eyes, they came walking close up to the sides of the *Astronef*. Some of them stroked her smooth, shining sides with their little hands, which Zaidie now found had only three fingers and a thumb. Many ages before they might have been bird's claws, but now they were soft and pink and plump, utterly strange to work as manual work is understood upon Earth.

"Just fancy getting Maxim guns ready to shoot those delightful things," said Zaidie, almost indignantly, as she went towards the doorway from which the gangway ladder ran down to the soft, mossy turf. "Why, not one of them has got a weapon of any sort; and just listen," she went on, stopping in the opening of the doorway, "have you ever heard music like that on earth? I haven't. I suppose it's the way they talk. I'd give a good deal to be able to understand them. But still, it's very lovely, isn't it?"

"Ay, like the voices of syrens," said Murgatroyd, speaking for the first time since the *Astronef* had landed; for this big, grizzled, taciturn Yorkshireman, who looked upon the whole cruise through Space as a mad and almost impious adventure, which nothing but his hereditary loyalty to his master's name and family could have persuaded him to share in, had grown more and more silent as the millions of miles between the *Astronef* and his native Yorkshire village had multiplied day by day.

"Syrens—and why not, Andrew?" laughed Redgrave. "At any rate, I don't think they look likely to lure us and the *Astronef* to destruction." Then he went on. "Yes, Zaidie, I never heard anything like that before. Unearthly, of course it is; but then we're not on Earth. Now, Zaidie, they seem to talk in song-language. You did pretty well on Mars with your sign-language, suppose we go out and show them that you can speak the song-language, too."

"What do you mean?" she said; "sing them something?"

"Yes," he replied, "they'll try to talk to you in song, and you won't be able to understand them; at least, not as far as words and sentences go. But music is the universal language on Earth, and there's no reason why it shouldn't be the same through the solar system. Come along, tune up, little woman!"

They went together down the gangway stairs, he dressed in an ordinary suit of grey English tweed, with a golf cap on the back of his head, and she in the last and daintiest of costumes which the art of Paris and London and New York had produced before the *Astronef* soared up from far-off Washington.

The moment that she set foot on the golden-yellow sward she was surrounded by a swarm of the winged, and yet strangely human creatures. Those nearest to her came and touched her hands and face, and stroked the folds of her dress. Others looked into her violet-blue eyes, and others put out their queer little hands and stroked her hair.

This and her clothing seemed to be the most wonderful experience for them, saving always the fact that she had two arms and no wings. Redgrave kept close beside her until he was satisfied that these exquisite inhabitants of the new-found fairyland were innocent of any intention of harm, and when he saw two of the winged daughters of the Love-Star put up their hands and touch the thick coils of her hair, he said:

"Take those pins and things out and let it down. They seem to think that your hair's part of your head. It's the first chance you've had to work a miracle, so you may as well do it. Show them the most beautiful thing they've ever seen."

"What babies you men can be when you get sentimental!" laughed Zaidie, as she put her hands up to her head. "How do you know that this may not be ugly in their eyes?"

"Quite impossible!" he replied. "They're a great deal too pretty themselves to think you ugly. Let it down!"

While he was speaking Zaidie had taken off a Spanish mantilla which she had thrown over her head as she came out, and which the ladies of Venus seemed to think was part of her hair. Then she took out the comb and one or two hairpins which kept the coils in position, deftly caught the ends, and then, after a few rapid movements of her fingers, she shook her head, and the wondering crowd about her saw, what seemed to them a shimmering veil, half gold, half silver, in the strange, reflected light from the cloud-veil, fall down from her head over her shoulders.

They crowded still more closely round her, but so quietly and so gently that she felt nothing more than the touch of wondering hands on her arms, and dress, and hair. As Redgrave said afterwards, he was "absolutely out of it." They seemed to imagine him to be a kind of uncouth monster, possibly the slave of this radiant being which had come so strangely from somewhere beyond the cloud-veil. They looked at him with their golden-yellow eyes wide open, and some of them came up rather timidly and touched his clothes, which they seemed to think were his skin.

Then one or two, more daring, put their little hands up to his face and touched his moustache, and all of them, while both examinations were going on, kept up a running conversation of cooing and singing which evidently conveyed their ideas from one to the other on the subject of this most marvellous visit of these two strange beings with neither wings nor feathers, but who, most undoubtedly, had other means of flying, since it was quite certain that they had come from another world.

Their ordinary speech was a low crooning note, like the language in which doves converse, mingled with a twittering current of undertone. But every moment it rose into higher notes, evidently expressing wonder or admiration, or both.

"You were right about the universal language," said Redgrave, when he had submitted to the stroking process for a few moments. "These people talk in music, and, as far as I can see or hear, their opinion of us, or, at least, of you, is distinctly flattering. I don't know what they take me for, and I don't care, but, as we'd better make friends with them, suppose you sing them 'Home, Sweet Home,' or 'The Swanee River.' I shouldn't wonder if they consider our talking voices most horrible discords, so you might as well give them something different."

While he was speaking the sounds about them suddenly hushed, and, as Redgrave said afterwards, it was something like the silence that follows a cannon shot. Then, in the midst of the hush, Zaidie put her hands behind her, looked up towards the luminous silver surface which formed the only visible sky of Venus, and began to sing "The Swanee River."

The clear, sweet notes rang up through the midst of a sudden silence. The sons and daughters of the Love-Star instantly ceased their own soft musical conversation, and Zaidie sang the old plantation song through for the first time that a human voice had sung it to ears other than human.

As the last note thrilled sweetly from her lips she looked round at the crowd of queer half-human figures about her, and something in their unlikeness to her own kind brought back to her mind the familiar scenes which lay so far away, so many millions of miles across the dark and silent Ocean of Space.

Other winged figures, attracted by the sound of her singing, had crossed the trees, and these, during the silence which came after the singing of the song, were swiftly followed by others, until there were nearly a thousand of them gathered about the side of the *Astronef.*

There was no crowding or jostling among them. Each one treated every other with the most perfect gentleness and courtesy. No such thing as enmity or ill-feeling seemed to exist among them, and, in perfect silence, they waited for Zaidie to continue what they thought was her long speech of greeting. The temper of the throng somehow coincided exactly with the mood which her own memories had brought to her, and the next moment she sent the first line of "Home Sweet Home" soaring up to the cloud-veiled sky.

As the notes rang up into the still, soft air a deeper hush fell on the listening throng. Heads were bowed with a gesture almost of adoration, and many of those standing nearest to her bent their bodies forward, and expanded their wings, bringing them together over their breasts with a motion which, as they afterwards learnt, was intended to convey the idea of wonder and admiration, mingled with something like a sentiment of worship.

Zaidie sang the sweet old song through from end to end, forgetting for the time being everything but the home she had left behind her on the banks of the Hudson. As the last notes left her lips, she turned round to Redgrave and looked at him with eyes dim with the first tears that had filled them since her father's death, and said, as he caught hold of her outstretched hand:

"I believe they've understood every word of it."

"Or, at any rate, every note. You may be quite certain of that," he replied. "If you had done that on Mars it might have been even more effective than the Maxims."

"For goodness sake don't talk about things like that in a heaven like this! Oh, listen! They've got the tune already!"

It was true! The dwellers of the Love-Star, whose speech was song, had instantly recognised the sweetness of the sweetest of all earthly songs. They had, of course, no idea of the meaning of the words; but the music spoke to them and told them that this fair visitant from another world could speak the same speech as theirs. Every note and cadence was repeated with absolute fidelity, and so the speech, common to the two far-distant worlds, became a link connecting this wandering son and daughter of the Earth with the sons and daughters of the Love-Star.

The throng fell back a little and two figures; apparently male and female, came to Zaidie and held out their right hands and began addressing her in perfectly harmonised song, which, though utterly unintelligible to her in the sense of speech, expressed sentiments which could not possibly be mistaken, as there was a faint suggestion of the old English song running through the little song-speech that they made, and both Zaidie and her husband rightly concluded that it was intended to convey a welcome to the strangers from beyond the cloud-veil.

And then the strangest of all possible conversations began. Redgrave, who had no more notion of music than a walrus, perforce kept silence. In fact, he noticed with a certain displeasure which vanished speedily with a musical and half-malicious little laugh from Zaidie, that when he spoke the Bird-Folk drew back a little and looked in something like astonishment at him; but Zaidie was already in touch with them, and half by song and half by signs she very soon gave them an idea of what they were and where they had come from. Her husband afterwards told her that it was the best piece of operatic acting he had ever seen, and, considering all the circumstances, this was very possibly true.

In the end the two, who had come to give her what seemed to be the formal greeting, were invited into the *Astronef*. They went on board without the slightest sign of mistrust, and with only an expression of mild wonder on their beautiful and strangely childlike faces.

Then, while the other doors were being closed, Zaidie stood at the open one above the gangway and made signs showing that they were going up beyond the clouds and then down into the valley, and as she made the signs she sang through the scale, her voice rising and falling in harmony with her gestures. The Bird-Folk understood her instantly, and as the door closed and the *Astronef* rose from the ground, a thousand wings were outspread and presently hundreds of beautiful soaring forms were circling about the Navigator of the Stars.

"Don't they look lovely!" said Zaidie. "I wonder what they would think if they could see us flying above New York or London or Paris with an escort like this. I suppose they're going to show us the way. Perhaps they have a city down there. Suppose you were to go and get a bottle of champagne and see if Master Cupid and Miss Venus would like a drink. We'll see then if our nectar is anything like theirs."

Redgrave went below. Meanwhile, for lack of other possible conversation, Zaidie began to sing the last verse of "Never Again." The melody almost exactly described the upward motion of the *Astronef*, and she could see that it was instantly understood, for when she had finished, their two voices joined in an almost exact

imitation of it.

When Redgrave brought up the wine and the glasses they looked at them without any sign of surprise. The pop of the cork did not even make them look round.

"Evidently a semi-angelic people, living on nectar and ambrosia, with nectar very like our own," he said, as he filled the glasses. "Perhaps you'd better give it to them. They seem to understand you better than they do me—you being, of course, a good bit nearer to the angels than I am."

"Thanks!" she said, as she took a couple of glasses up, wondering a little what their visitors would do with them. Somewhat to her surprise, they took them with a little bow and a smile and sipped at the wine, first with a swift glint of wonder in their eyes, and then with smiles which are unmistakable evidence of perfect appreciation.

"I thought so," said Redgrave, as he raised his own glass, and bowed gravely towards them. "This is our nearest approach to nectar, and they seem to recognise it."

"And don't they just look like the sort of people who live on it, and, of course, other things?" added Zaidie, as she too lifted her glass, and looked with laughing eyes across the brim at her two guests.

But meanwhile Murgatroyd had been applying the repulsive force a little too strongly. The *Astronef* shot up with a rapidity which soon left her winged escort far below. She entered the cloud-veil and passed beyond it. The instant that the unclouded sun-rays struck the glass-roofing of the upper deck, their two guests, who had been moving about examining everything with a childlike curiosity, closed their eyes and clasped their hands over them, uttering little cries, tuneful and musical, but still with a note of strange discord in them.

"Lenox, we must go down again," exclaimed Zaidie. "Don't you see they can't stand the light; it hurts them. Perhaps, poor dears, it's the first time they've ever been hurt in their lives. I don't believe they have any of our ideas of pain or sorrow or anything of that sort. Take us back under the clouds—quick, or we may blind them."

Before she had finished speaking, Redgrave had sent a signal down to Murgatroyd, and the *Astronef* began to drop back again towards the surface of the cloud-sea. Zaidie had, meanwhile, gone to her lady guest and dropped the black lace mantilla over her head, and, as she did so, she caught herself saying:

"There, dear, we shall soon be back in your own light. I hope it hasn't hurt you. It was very stupid of us to do a thing like that."

The answer came in a little cooing murmur, which said, "Thank you!" quite as effectively as any earthly words could have done, and then the *Astronef* dropped through the cloud-sea. The soaring forms of her lost escort came into view again and clustered about her; and, surrounded by them, she dropped, in obedience to their signs, down between the tremendous mountains and towards the island, thick with golden foliage, which lay two or three earth-miles out in a bay, where four converging rivers spread out into the sea.

As Lady Redgrave said afterwards to Mrs. Van Stuyler, she could have filled a whole volume with a description of the purely Arcadian delights with which the hours of the next ten days and nights were filled. Possibly if she had been able to do justice to them, even her account might have been received with qualified credence; but still some idea of them may be gathered from this extract of a conversation which took place in the saloon of the

Astronef on the eleventh evening.

"But look here, Zaidie," said his lordship, "as we've found a world which is certainly much more delightful than our own, why shouldn't we stop here a bit? The air suits us and the people are simply enchanting. I think they like us, and I'm sure you're in love with every one of them, male and female. Of course, it's rather a pity that we can't fly unless we do it in the *Astronef*. But that's only a detail. You're enjoying yourself thoroughly, and I never saw you looking better or, if possible, more beautiful; and why on earth —- or Venus—do you want to go?"

She looked at him steadily for a few moments, and with an expression which he had never seen on her face or in her eyes before, and then she said slowly and very sweetly, although there was something like a note of solemnity running through her tone:

"I altogether agree with you, dear; but there is something which you don't seem to have noticed. As you say, we have had a perfectly delightful time. It's a delicious world, and just everything that one would think it to be; but if we were to stop here we should be committing one of the greatest crimes, perhaps the greatest, that ever was committed within the limits of the Solar System."

"My dear Zaidie, what in the name of what we used to call morals on the earth, do you mean?"

"Just this," she replied, leaning a little towards him in her deck-chair. "These people, half angels, and half men and women, welcomed us after we dropped through their cloud-veil, as friends; we were a little strange to them, certainly, but still they welcomed us as friends. They had no suspicions of us; they didn't try to poison us or blow us up as those wretches on Mars did. They're just like a lot of grown-up children with wings on. In fact they're about as nearly angels as anything we can think of. They've taken us into their palaces, they've given us, as one might say, the whole planet. Everything was ours that we liked to take. You know we have two or three hundredweight of precious stones on board now, which they would make me take just because they saw my rings.

"We've been living with them ten days now, and neither you nor I, nor even Murgatroyd, who, like the old Puritan that he is, seems to see sin or wrong in everything that looks nice, has seen a single sign among them that they know anything about what we call sin or wrong on Earth. There's no jealousy, no selfishness. In short, no envy, hatred, malice, and all uncharitableness; no vice, or meanness, or cheating, or any of the abominations of the planet Terra, and we come from that planet. Do you see what I mean now?"

"I think I understand what you're driving at," said Redgrave. "You mean, I suppose, that this world is something like Eden before the fall, and that you and I—oh—but that's all rubbish you know. I've got my own share of original sin, of course, but here it doesn't seem to come in; and as for you, the very idea of you imagining yourself a feminine edition of the Serpent in Eden. Nonsense!"

She got up out of her chair and, leaning over his, put her arm round his shoulder. Then she said very softly:

"I see you understand what I mean, Lenox. That's just it—original sin. It doesn't matter how good you think me or I think you, but we have it. You're an Earth-born man and I'm an earth-born woman, and, as I'm your wife, I can say it plainly. We may think a good bit of each other, but that's no reason why we shouldn't be a couple of plague-spots in a sinless world like this. Surely you see what I mean, I needn't put it plainer, need I?"

Their eyes met, and he read her meaning in hers. He put his arm up over her shoulder and drew her down towards him. Their lips met, and then he got up and went down to the engine-room.

A couple of minutes later the *Astronef* sprang upwards from the midst of the delightful valley in which she was resting. No lights were shown. In five minutes she had passed through the cloud-veil, and the next morning when their new friends came to visit them and found that they had vanished back into Space, there was sorrow for the first time among the sons and daughters of the Love-Star.

Chapter 14

FIVE HUNDRED MILLION miles from the earth and forty-seven million miles from Jupiter," said his lordship, as he came into breakfast on the morning of the twenty-eighth day after leaving Venus.

During this brief period the *Astronef* had recrossed the orbits of the Earth and Mars and passed through that marvellous region of the Solar System, the Belt of the Asteroides. Nearly a hundred million miles of their journey had lain through this zone in which hundreds and possibly thousands of tiny planets revolve in vast orbits round the Sun.

Then had come a worldless void of over three hundred million miles, through which the *Astronef* voyaged alone, surrounded by the ever-constant splendours of the Heavens, but visited only now and then by one of those Spectres of Space, which we call comets.

Astern, the disc of the Sun steadily diminished, and ahead the grey-blue shape of Jupiter, the Giant of the Solar System, had grown larger and larger until now they could see it as it had never been seen before—a gigantic three-quarter moon filling up the whole Heavens in front of them almost from Zenith to Nadir. Three of its four satellites, Europa, Ganymede, and Calisto were distinctly visible to the naked eye, and Europa and Ganymede, happened to be in such a position with regard to the *Astronef* that her crew could see not only the bright sides turned towards the sun, but also the black shadow-spots which they cast on the cloud-veiled face of the huge planet. Calisto was above the horizon hanging like a tiny flicker of yellowish-red light above the rounded edge of Jupiter, and Io was invisible behind the planet.

"Five hundred million miles!" said Zaidie, with a little shiver, "that seems an awful long way from home—I mean America—doesn't it? I often wonder what they are thinking about us on the dear old Earth. I don't suppose anyone ever expects to see us again. However, it's no good getting homesick in the middle of a journey when you're outward bound. And now what is the program as regards His Majesty King Jove? We shall visit the satellites of course?"

"Certainly," replied Redgrave; "in fact, I shouldn't be surprised if our visit was confined to them."

"What! Do you mean to say we shan't land on Jupiter after coming nearly six hundred million miles to see him? That would be disappointing. But why not? don't you think he's ready to be visited yet?"

"I can't say that, but you must remember that no one has the remotest notion of what there is behind the clouds or whatever they are which form those bands. All we really know about Jupiter is his enormous size, for instance, he's over twelve hundred times bigger than the Earth and that his density isn't much greater than that of water—and my humble opinion is that if we're able to go through the clouds without getting the *Astronef* red-hot we shall find that Jupiter is in the same state as the Earth was a good many million years ago."

"I see," said Zaidie, "you mean just a mass of blazing, boiling rock and metal which will make islands and continents some day; and that what we call the cloud bands are the vapours which will one day make its seas. Well, if we can get through these clouds we ought to see something worth seeing. Just fancy a whole world as big as that all ablaze like molten iron! Do you think we shall be able to see it, Lenox?"

"I'm not so sure about that, little woman. We shall have to go to work rather cautiously. You see Jupiter is far bigger than any world we've visited yet, and if we get too close to him the *Astronef*'s engines might not be powerful enough to drive us away again. Then we should either stop there till the R. Force was exhausted or be drawn towards him and perhaps drop into an ocean of molten rock and metal."

"Thanks!" said Zaidie, with a shrug of her shapely shoulders. "That would be an ignominious end to a journey like this, to say nothing of the boiling oil part of it; so I suppose you'll make stopping-places of the satellites and use their attraction to help you resist His Majesty's."

"Your Ladyship's reasoning is perfect. I propose to visit them in turn, beginning with Calisto. I shouldn't be at all surprised if we found something interesting on them. You know they're quite little worlds of themselves. They're all bigger than our moon, except Europa. Ganymede, in fact, is two-thirds bigger than Mercury, and if old Jupiter is still in a state of fiery incandescence there's no reason why we shouldn't find on Ganymede or one of the others the same state of things that existed on our moon when the Earth was blazing hot."

"I shouldn't wonder," said Zaidie; "I've often heard my father say that that was probably what happened. It's all very marvellous, isn't it? death in one place, life in another, all beginnings and endings, and yet no actual beginning or end of anything anywhere. That's eternity, I suppose."

"It's just about as near as the finite intellect can get to it, I should say," replied Redgrave. "But I don't think metaphysics are much in our line. If you've finished we may as well go and have a look at the realities."

"Which the metaphysicians," laughed Zaidie as she rose, "would tell you are not realities at all, or only realities so far as you can think about them. 'Thinks,' in short, instead of real things. But meanwhile I've got the breakfast things to put away, so you can go up on deck and put the telescopes in order."

When she joined him a few minutes later in the deck-chamber the three-quarter disc of Jupiter was rapidly approaching the full.

Its phases are invisible from the Earth owing to the enormous distance; but from the deck of the *Astronef* they had been plainly visible for some days, and, since the huge planet turns on its axis in less than ten hours, or with more than twice the speed of the Earth's rotation, the phases followed each other very rapidly.

Thus at twelve o'clock noon by *Astronef* time they might have seen a gigantic rim of silver-blue over-arching the whole vault of heaven in front of them. By five o'clock it would be a hemisphere, and by five minutes to ten the vast sphere would be once more shining full-orbed upon them. By eight o'clock next morning they would find Jupiter "new" again.

They were now falling very rapidly towards the huge planet, and, since there is no up or down in Space, the nearer they got to it the more it appeared to sink below them and become, as it were, the floor of the Celestial Sphere. As the crescent approached the full they were able to examine the mysterious bands as human observers had never examined them before. For hours they sat almost silent at their telescopes, trying to probe the mystery which has baffled human science since the days of Galileo, and gradually it became plain that Redgrave was correct in the hypothesis which he had derived from Flammarion and one or two others of the more advanced astronomers.

"I believe I was right, or, in other words, those that I got the idea from are," he said, as they approached the orbit of Calisto, which revolves at a distance of about eleven hundred thousand miles from the surface of Jupiter.

"Those belts are made of clouds or vapour in some stage or other. The highest—the ones along the Equator and what we should call the Temperate Zones—are the highest, and therefore coolest and whitest. The dark ones are the lowest and hottest. I daresay they are more like what we should call volcanic clouds. Do you see how they keep changing? That's what's bothered our astronomers. Look at that big one yonder a bit to the north, going from brown to red. I suppose that's something like the famous red spot which they have been puzzling about. What do you make of it?"

"Well," said Zaidie, looking up from her telescope, "it's quite certain that the glare must come from underneath. It can't be sunlight, because the poor old Sun doesn't seem to have strength enough to make a decent sunset or sunrise here, and look how it's running along to the westward! What does that mean, do you think?"

"I should say it means that some half-formed Jovian Continent has been flung sky high by a big burst-up underneath, and that's the blaze of the incandescent stuff running along. Just fancy a continent, say ten times the size of Asia, being split up and sent flying in a few moments like that! Look! there's another one to the north! On the whole, dear, I don't think we should find the climate on the other side of those clouds very salubrious. Still, as they say the atmosphere of Jupiter is about ten thousand miles thick, we may be able to get near enough to see something of what's going on.

"Meanwhile, here comes Calisto. Look at his shadow flying across the clouds. And there's Ganymede coming up after him, and Europa behind him. Talk about eclipses! they must be about as common here as thunderstorms are with us."

"We don't have a thunderstorm every day—at least not at home," corrected Zaidie, "but on Jupiter they must have two or three eclipses every day Meanwhile, there goes Jupiter himself. What a difference distance makes! This little thing is only a trifle larger than our Moon, and it's hiding everything else."

As she was speaking the full-orbed disc of Calisto, measuring nearly three thousand miles across, swept between them and the planet. It shone with a clear, somewhat reddish light like that of Mars. The *Astronef* was feeling his attraction strongly, and Redgrave went to the levers and turned on about a fifth of the R. Force to avoid too sudden contact with it.

"Another dead world!" said Redgrave, as the surface of Calisto revolved swiftly beneath them, "or at any rate a dying one. There must be an atmosphere of some sort, or else that snow and ice wouldn't be there, and everything would be either black or white as it was on the Moon. We may as well land, however, and get a specimen of the rocks and soil to add to the museum, though I don't expect there will be very much to see in the way of life."

In another hour or so the *Astronef* had dropped gently on to the surface of Calisto at the foot of a range of mountains crowded with jagged and splintery peaks, and a mile or two from the edge of a sea of snow and ice which stretched away in a vast expanse of rugged frozen billows beyond the horizon. Redgrave, as usual, went into the air-chamber and tried the atmosphere. A second's experience of it was enough for him. It was unbreathably thin and unbearably cold, although, when mixed with the air of the *Astronef*, it distinctly freshened it up. This proved that its composition was, or had been, fit for human respiration.

"There's only one fault about it," he said, when he rejoined Zaidie in the sitting-room. "You know what the schoolboy said when he started kissing his first sweetheart, 'It takes too long to get enough of it.'"

"You seem to be very fond of referring to that particular subject, Lenox."

"Well, yes; to tell you the truth I am," and then he referred to it again in another form.

After this they went and put on their breathing-dresses and went for a welcome stroll along the arid shores of the frozen sea after their lengthy confinement to the decks of the *Astronef*. The Sun was still powerful enough to keep them comfortably warm in their dresses, and there was enough atmosphere to make this warmth diffused instead of direct. So they were able to step out briskly, and every now and then open their visors a little and take in a breath or two of the thin, sharp air, which they found quite exhilarating when mixed with the air supplied by their own oxygen apparatus.

The attraction of the satellite being only a little more than that of the Moon—or, say, about a fifth of that of the Earth—they were able to get along with a series of hops, skips, and jumps which might have looked rather ridiculous to terrestrial eyes, but which they found a very pleasant mode of locomotion. They were also able to climb the steepest mountainsides with no more trouble than they would have had in walking along a terrestrial plain.

On the heights they found no sign either of animal or vegetable life—only rocks and gravel and sand of a brownish red, apparently uniform in composition. They took a few lumps of rock and a canvas bag full of sand back with them from the mountain-side. In the valley sloping towards the ice sea they found what had once been watercourses opening out into rivers towards the sea; and in the lowest parts there was a kind of lichen-growth clinging to the rocks under the snow. On the surface of the snow they saw traces of what might have been the tracks of animals, but, as there was no breath of wind in the attenuated atmosphere, it was quite possible that these might have been frozen into permanent shape hundreds or thousands of years before. It was also possible that if they had explored long enough they might have found some low forms of animal life, but as they had landed almost on the equator of the satellite, under the full rays of the Sun, and seen nothing, this was hardly likely.

"I don't think it is worth while stopping here any longer," said Zaidie, who was getting a little bit blase with her interplanetary experiences. "We've got lots to see further on, so if you don't mind I think I'll just take two or three photographs, then we can get back to the ship and have dinner and go on and see what Ganymede is like. He's bigger than Mercury, and nearly as big as Mars, so we ought to find something interesting there. This is only a sort of combination of the Moon and the polar regions and I don't think very much of it. Suppose we go back."

"Just as your Ladyship pleases," laughed Redgrave over the wire which connected their helmets, as, with joined hands, they turned back and danced along the snow-covered ocean shore towards the *Astronef.*

Zaidie took a couple of photographs of the mountain range and the ice-sea and another one of the general landscape of Calisto as they rose from the surface. Then, while she went to get lunch ready, Redgrave took the pieces of rock and the bag of dust into the laboratory which opened out of the main engine-room and analysed them. When he came out about an hour later he saw Murgatroyd going through his beloved engines with an oil-can and a piece of common cotton-waste which had come from a far away Yorkshire mill.

"Andrew," he said, "should you be surprised if I told you that that moon we've just left seems to be mostly made of a spongy sort of alloy of gold and silver?"

"My lord," said the old engineer, straightening himself up and looking at him with eyes in which this announcement had not seemed to kindle a spark of interest, "after what I have seen so far there's nothing that'll surprise me unless it be that the grace of God allows us to get back safely."

"Amen, Andrew, that's well said," replied Redgrave, and then he went back to the saloon and Murgatroyd went on with his oiling.

When he told her ladyship of his discovery she just looked up from the table she was laying and said:

"Oh, indeed! Well, I'm very glad that it's five or six hundred million miles from the Earth. A dead world bigger than the Moon, and made of gold and silver sponge, wouldn't be a nice thing to have too near the Earth. There's trouble enough about that sort of thing at home as it is. Still, it'll be a nice addition to the museum, and if you'll put it away and go and wash your hands lunch will be ready."

When they got back to the deck-chamber Calisto was already a half moon in the upper sky nearly five hundred thousand miles away, and the full orb of Ganymede, shining with a pale golden light, lay outspread beneath them. A thin, bluish-grey arc of the giant planet overarched its western edge.

"I think we shall find something like a world here," said her ladyship, when she had taken her first look through her telescope; "there's an atmosphere and what look like thin clouds. Continents and oceans too, or something like them, and what is that light shining up between the breaks? Isn't it something like our Aurora?"

"It might be," replied Redgrave, turning his own telescope towards the northern pole of Ganymede, "though I never heard of a satellite having an aurora. Perhaps it's the Sun shining on the ice."

As the *Astronef* fell towards the surface of Ganymede she crossed his northern pole, and the nearer they got the plainer it became that a light very like the terrestrial Aurora was playing about it, illuminating the thin, yellow clouds with a bluish-violet light, which made magnificent contrasts of colouring amongst them.

"Let us go down there and see what it's like," said Zaidie.

"There must be something nice under all those lovely colours."

Redgrave checked the R. Force and the *Astronef* fell obliquely across the pole towards the equator. As they approached the luminous clouds Redgrave turned it on again, and they sank slowly through a glowing mist of innumerable colours, until the surface of Ganymede came into plain view about ten miles below them.

What they saw then was the strangest sight they had beheld since they had left the Earth. As far as their eyes could reach the surface of the Ganymede was covered with vast orderly patches, mostly rectangular, of what they at first took for ice, but which they soon found to be a something that was self-illuminating.

"Glorified hot-houses, as I'm alive," exclaimed Redgrave. "Whole cities under glass, fields, too, and lit by electricity or something very like it. Zaidie, we shall find human beings down there."

"Well, if we do I hope they won't be like the half-human things we found on Mars! But isn't it all just lovely! Only there doesn't seem to be anything outside the cities, at least nothing but bare, flat ground with a few rugged mountains here and there. See, there's a nice level plain near the big glass city, or whatever it is. Suppose we go down there."

Redgrave checked the after-engine which was driving them obliquely over the surface of the satellite, and the *Astronef* fell vertically towards a bare flat plain of what looked like deep yellow sand, which spread for miles alongside one of the glittering cities of glass.

"Oh, look, they've seen us!" exclaimed Zaidie. "I do hope they're going to be as friendly as those dear people on Venus were."

"I hope so," replied Redgrave, "but if they're not we've got the guns ready."

As he said this about twenty streams of an intense bluish light suddenly shot up all round them, concentrating themselves upon the hull of the *Astronef*, which was now about a mile and a half from the surface. The light was so intense that the rays of the Sun were lost in it. They looked at each other, and found that their faces were almost perfectly white in it. The plain and the city below had vanished.

To look downwards was like staring straight into the focus of a ten thousand candlepower electric arc lamp. It was so intolerable that Redgrave closed the lower shutters, and meanwhile he found that the *Astronef* had ceased to descend. He shut off more of the R. force, but it produced no effect. The *Astronef* remained stationary. Then he ordered Murgatroyd to set the propellers in motion. The engineer pulled the starting levers, and then came up out of the engine-room and said to him:

"It's no good my lord; I don't know what devil's world we've got into now, but they won't work. If I thought that engines could be bewitched—"

"Oh, nonsense, Andrew!" said his lordship rather testily. "It's perfectly simple; those people down there, whoever they are, have got some way of demagnetising us, or else they've got the R. Force too, and they're applying it against us to stop us going down. Apparently they don't want us. No, that's just to show us that they can stop us if they want to. The light's going down. Begin dropping a bit. Don't start the propellers, but just go and see that the guns are all right in case of accidents."

The old engineer nodded and went back to his engines, looking considerably scared. As he spoke the brilliancy of the light faded rapidly and the *Astronef* began to sink slowly towards the surface.

As a precaution against their being allowed to drop with force enough to cause a disaster, Redgrave turned the R. Force on again and they dropped slowly towards the plain, through what seemed like a halo of perfectly white light. When she was within a couple of hundred yards of the ground a winged car of exquisitely graceful shape rose from the roof of one of the huge glass buildings nearest to them, flew swiftly towards them, and after circling once round the dome of the upper deck, ran close alongside.

The car was occupied by two figures of distinctly human form but rather more than human stature. Both were dressed in long, close-fitting garments of what seemed like a golden brown fleece. Their heads were covered with a close hood and their hands with thin, close-fitting gloves.

"What an exceedingly handsome man!" said Zaidie, as one of

them stood up. "I never saw such a noble-looking face in my life; it's half philosopher, half saint. Of course, you won't be jealous."

"Oh, nonsense!" he laughed. "It would be quite impossible to imagine you in love with either. But he is handsome, and evidently friendly—there's no mistaking that. Answer him, Zaidie; you can do it better than I can."

The car had now come close alongside. The standing figure stretched its hands out, palms upward, smiled a smile which Zaidie thought was very sweetly solemn, next the head was bowed, and the gloved hands brought back and crossed over his breast. Zaidie imitated the movements exactly. Then, as the figure raised its head, she raised hers, and she found herself looking into a pair of large luminous eyes, such as she could have imagined under the brows of an angel. As they met hers, a look of unmistakable wonder and admiration came into them. Redgrave was standing just behind her; she took him by the hand and drew him beside her, saying with a little laugh:

"Now, please look as pleasant as you can; I am sure they are very friendly. A man with a face like that couldn't mean any harm."

The figure repeated the motions to Redgrave, who returned them, perhaps a trifle awkwardly. Then the car began to descend, and the figure beckoned to them to follow.

"You'd better go and wrap up, dear. From the gentleman's dress it seems pretty cold outside, though the air is evidently quite breathable," said Redgrave, as the *Astronef* began to drop in company with the car. "At any rate, I'll try it first, and, if it isn't, we can put on our breathing-dresses."

When Zaidie had made her winter toilet, and Redgrave had found the air to be quite respirable, but of Arctic cold, they went down the gangway ladder about twenty minutes later.

The figure had got out of the car which was lying a few yards from them on the sandy plain, and came forward to meet them with both hands outstretched .

Zaidie unhesitatingly held out hers, and a strange thrill ran through her as she felt them for the first time clasped gently by other than earthly hands, for the Venus folk had only been able to pat and stroke with their gentle little paws, somewhat as a kitten might do. The figure bowed its head again and said something in a low, melodious voice, which was, of course, quite unintelligible save for the evident friendliness of its tone. Then, releasing her hands, he took Redgrave's in the same fashion, and then led the way towards a vast, domed building of semi-opaque glass, or rather a substance which seemed to be something like a mixture of glass and mica, which appeared to be one of the entrance gates of the city.

CHAPTER 15

THE WONDERING VISITORS from far-off Terra had hardly halted before the magnificent portal when a huge sheet of frosted glass rose silently from the ground. They passed through, and it fell behind them. They found themselves in a great oval antechamber along each side of which stood triple rows of strangely shaped trees whose leaves gave off a subtle and most agreeable scent. The temperature here was several degrees higher, in fact about that of an English spring day, and Zaidie immediately threw open her big fur cloak saying:

"These good people seem to live in Winter Gardens, don't they? I don't think I shall want these things much while we're inside. I wonder what dear old Andrew would have thought of this if we could have persuaded him to leave the ship."

They followed their host through the antechamber towards a magnificent pointed arch raised on clusters of small pillars each of a different coloured, highly polished stone, which shone brilliantly in a light which seemed to come from nowhere. Another door, this time of pale, transparent, blue glass, rose as they approached; they passed under it and, as it fell behind them, half-a-dozen figures, considerably shorter and slighter than their host, came forward to meet them. He took off his gloves and cape and thick outer covering, and they were glad to follow his example for the atmosphere was now that of a warm June day.

The attendants, as they evidently were, took their wraps from them, looking at the furs and stroking them with evident wonder; but with nothing like the wonder which came into their wild, soft grey eyes when they looked at Zaidie, who, as usual when she arrived on a new world, was arrayed in one of her daintiest costumes.

Their host was now dressed in a tunic of a light blue material, which glistened with a lustre greater than that of the finest silk. It reached a little below his knees, and was confined at the waist by a sash of the same colour hut of somewhat deeper hue. His feet and legs were covered with stockings of the same material and colour, and his feet, which were small for his stature and exquisitely shaped, were shod with thin sandals of a material which looked like soft felt, and which made no noise as he walked over the delicately coloured mosaic pavement of the street—for such it actually was—which ran past the gate.

When he removed his cap they expected to find that he was bald like the Martians, but they were mistaken. His well-shaped head was covered with long, thick hair of a colour something between bronze and grey. A broad band of metal looking like light gold passed round the upper part of his forehead, and from under this the hair fell in gentle waves to below his shoulders.

For a few moments Zaidie and Redgrave stared about them in frank and silent wonder. They were standing in a broad street running in a straight line to what seemed to be several miles along the edge of a city of crystal. It was lined with double rows of trees with beds of brilliantly coloured flowers between them. From this street others went off at right angles and at regular intervals. The roof of the city appeared to be composed of an infinity of domes of enormous extent, supported by tall clusters of slender pillars standing at the street corners. The general level of the roof seemed to be about three hundred feet above the ground, and the summits of the domes some fifty feet higher.

The houses, which were all square, were as a rule about forty feet high. The roofs were covered with gardens and shrubberies, from which creepers, bearing brilliantly coloured leaves and flowers, hung down about the windows in carefully arranged festoons. The walls were composed of the opaque mica-like glass, relieved by pillars and arched doorways and windows. The windows, of French form, were of clear glass and mostly stood open. A sweet cool zephyr of hardly perceptible strength appeared to be blowing along the street and over the house-tops and in the vast airy space above the roof.

Brightly plumaged birds were flitting about among the branches of giant trees, and keeping up a perpetual chorus of song.

Presently their host touched Redgrave on the shoulder and pointed to a four-wheeled car of light framework and exquisite design, containing seats for four besides the driver, or guide, who sat behind. He held out his hand to Zaidie, and handed her to one of the front seats just as an earth-born gentleman might have done. Then he motioned to Redgrave to sit beside her, and mounted behind them.

The car immediately began to move silently, but with considerable speed, along the left-hand side of the outer street, which, like all the others, was divided by narrow strips of russet-coloured grass and flowering shrubs.

In a few minutes it swung round to the right, crossed the road, and entered a magnificent avenue, which, after a run of some four miles, ended in a vast, park-like square, measuring at least a mile each way.

The two sides of the avenue were busy with cars like their own, some carrying six people, and others only the driver. Those on each side of the road all went in the same direction. Those nearest to the broad side-walks between the houses and the first row of trees went at a moderate speed of five or six miles an hour, but along the inner sides, near the central line of trees, they seemed to be running as high as thirty miles an hour. Their occupants were nearly all dressed in clothes made of the same glistening, silky fabric as their host wore, but the colourings were of infinite variety.

It was quite easy to distinguish between the sexes, although in stature they were almost equal. The men were nearly all clothed as their host was. The colours of their garments were quieter, and there was little attempt at personal adornment, though many wore bands of an intensely bright, sky-blue metal round their arms above the elbow, and others wore belts and necklaces of links composed of this and two other metals resembling gold and aluminium, but of an exceedingly high lustre.

The women were dressed in flowing garments something after the Greek style, but they were of brighter hues, and much more lavishly embroidered than the men's tunics were. They also wore much more jewellery. Indeed, some of the younger ones glittered from head to foot with polished metal and gleaming stones. There was one more difference which they quickly noticed. The men's hair, like their host's, was nearly always wavy, but that of the women, especially the younger, was a mass of either natural or artificial curls, short and crisp about the head, and flowing down in glistening ringlets to their waists.

"Could anyone ever have dreamt of such a lovely place?" said Zaidie, after their wondering eyes had become accustomed to the marvels about them, "and yet— oh dear, now I know what it reminds me of! Flammarion's book, 'The End Of The World,' where he describes the remnants of the human race dying of cold and hunger on the Equator in places something like this. I suppose the life of poor Ganymede is giving out, and that's why they've got to live in glorified Crystal Palaces like this, poor things."

"Poor things!" laughed Redgrave, "I'm afraid I can't agree with you there, dear. I never saw a jollier looking lot of people in my life. I daresay you're quite right, but they certainly seem to view their approaching end with considerable equanimity."

"Don't be horrid, Lenox! Fancy talking in that cold-blooded way about such delightful-looking people as these, why, they are even nicer than our dear bird-folk on Venus, and, of course, they are a great deal more like ourselves."

"Wherefore it stands to reason that they must be a great deal nicer!" he replied, with a glance which brought a brighter flush to her cheeks. Then he went on: "Ah, now I see the difference."

"What difference? Between what?"

"Between the daughter of Earth and the daughters of Ganymede," he replied. "You can blush, and I don't think they can. Haven't you noticed that, although they have the most exquisite skins and beautiful eyes and hair and all that sort of thing, not a man or woman of them has any colouring. I suppose that's the result of living for generations in a hothouse."

"Very likely," she said; "but has it struck you also that all the girls and women are either beautiful or handsome, and all the men, except the ones who seem to be servants or slaves, are something like Greek gods, or, at least, the sort of men you see on the Greek sculptures?"

"Survival of the fittest, I presume. These will be the descendants of the highest races of Ganymede; the people who conceived the idea of prolonging the life of their race and were able to carry it out. The inferior races would either perish of starvation or become their servants. That's what will happen on Earth, and there is no reason why it shouldn't have happened here."

As he said this the car swung out round a broad curve into the centre of the great square, and a little cry of amazement broke from Zaidie's lips as her glance roamed over the multiplying splendours about her.

In the centre of the square, in the midst of smooth lawns and flower beds of every conceivable shape and colour, and groves of flowering trees, stood a great, domed building, which they approached through an avenue of overarching trees interlaced with flowering creepers.

The car stopped at the foot of a triple flight of stairs of dazzling whiteness which led up to a broad, arched doorway. Several groups of people were sprinkled about the avenue and steps and the wide terrace which ran along the front of the building. They looked with keen, but perfectly well-mannered surprise at their strange visitors, and seemed to be discussing their appearance; but not a step was taken towards them nor was there the slightest sign of anything like vulgar curiosity.

"What perfect manners these dear people have!" said Zaidie, as they dismounted at the foot of the staircase. "I wonder what would happen if a couple of them were to be landed from a motor car in front of the Capitol at Washington. I suppose this is their Capitol, and we've been brought here to be put through our facings. What a pity we can't talk to them. I wonder if they'd believe our story if we could tell it."

"I've no doubt they know something of it already," replied Redgrave; "they're evidently people of immense intelligence. Intellectually, I daresay, we're mere children compared with them, and it's quite possible that they have developed senses which we have no idea of."

"And perhaps," added Zaidie, "all the time that we are talking to each other our friend here is quietly reading everything that is going on in our minds."

Whether this was so or not their host gave no sign of comprehension. He led them up the steps and through the great doorway, where he was met by three splendidly dressed men even taller than himself.

"I feel beastly shabby among all these gorgeously attired personages," said Redgrave, looking down at his plain tweed suit, as they were conducted with every manifestation of politeness along the magnificent vestibule into which the door opened.

"And I'm sure that I am quite a dowdy in comparison with these lovely creatures," added Zaidie, "although this dress was made in Paris. Lenox, if things are for sale here you'll have to buy me one of those costumes, and we'll take it back and get one made like it. I wonder what they'd think of me dressed in one of those costumes at a ball at the Wardolf-Astoria."

Before he could make a suitable reply, a door at the end of the vestibule opened and they were ushered into a large hall which was evidently a council-chamber. At the further end of it were three semicircular rows of seats made of the polished silvery metal, and in the centre and raised slightly above them another under a canopy of sky-blue silk. This seat and six others were occupied by men of most venerable aspect, in spite of the fact that their hair was just as long and thick and glossy as their host's or even as Zaidie's own.

The ceremony of introduction was exceedingly simple. Though they could not, of course, understand a word he said, it was evident from his eloquent gestures that their host described the way in which they had come from Space, and landed on the surface of the World of the Crystal Cities, as Zaidie subsequently rechristened Ganymede.

The President of the Senate or Council spoke a few sentences in a deep musical tone. Then their host, taking their hands, led them up to his seat, and the the President rose and took them by both hands in turn. Then, with a grave smile of greeting, he bent his head and resumed his seat. They joined hands in turn with each of the six senators present, bowed their farewells in silence, and then went back with their host to the car.

They ran down the avenue, made a curving sweep round to the left—for all the paths in the great square were laid in curves, apparently to form a contrast to the straight streets—and presently stopped before the porch of one of the hundred palaces which surrounded it. This was their host's house, and their home during the rest of their sojourn on Ganymede.

CHAPTER 16

THE PERIOD OF GANYMEDE'S revolution round its gigantic primary is seven days, three hours, and forty-three minutes, practically a terrestrial week, and on their return to their native world both the daring navigators of Space describe this as the most interesting and delightful week in their lives, excepting always the period which they spent in the Eden of the Morning Star. Yet in one sense it was even more interesting.

There the inhabitants had never learnt to sin; here they had learnt the lesson that sin is mere foolishness, and that no really sensible or properly educated man or woman thinks crime worth committing.

The life of the Crystal Cities, of which they visited four in different parts of the satellite, using the *Astronef* as their vehicle, was one of peaceful industry and calm innocent enjoyment. It was quite plain that their first impressions of this aged world were correct. Outside the cities spread a universal desert on which life was impossible. There was hardly any moisture in the thin atmosphere. The rivers had dwindled into rivulets and the seas into vast, shallow marshes. The heat received from the Sun was only about a twenty-fifth of that which falls on the surface of the Earth, and this was drawn to the cities and collected and preserved under their glass domes by a number of devices which displayed superhuman intelligence.

The dwindling supplies of water were hoarded in vast subterranean reservoirs and, by means of a perfect system of redistillation, the priceless fluid was used over and over again both for human purposes and for irrigating the land within the cities. Still the total quantity was steadily diminishing, for it was not only evaporating from the surface, but, as the orb cooled more and more rapidly towards its centre, it descended deeper and deeper below the surface, and could now only be reached by means of marvellously constructed borings and pumping machinery which extended down several miles into the ground.

The fast-failing store of heat in the centre of the little world, which had now cooled through more than half its bulk, was utilised for warming the air of the cities, and to drive the machinery which propelled it through the streets and squares. All work was done by electric energy developed directly from this source, which also actuated the repulsive engines which had prevented the *Astronef* from descending.

In short, the inhabitants of Ganymede were engaged in a steady, ceaseless struggle to utilise the expiring natural forces of their world to prolong their own lives and the exquisitely refined civilisation to which they had attained to the latest possible date. They were, indeed, in exactly the same position in which the distant descendants of the human race may one day be expected to find themselves.

Their domestic life, as Zaidie and Lenox saw it while they were the guests of their host, was the perfection of simplicity and comfort, and their public life was characterised by a quiet but intense intellectuality which, as Zaidie had said, made them feel very much like children who had only just learnt to speak.

As they possessed magnificent telescopes, far surpassing any on earth, the wanderers were able to survey, not only the Solar System, but the other systems far beyond its limits as no other of their kind had ever been able to do before. They did not look through or into the telescopes. The lens was turned upon the object, which was thrown, enormously magnified, upon screens of what looked something like ground glass some fifty feet square. It was thus that they saw, not only the whole visible surface of Jupiter as he revolved above them and they about him, but also their native Earth, sometimes a pale silver disc or crescent close to the edge of the Sun, visible only in the morning and the evening of Jupiter, and at other times like a little black spot crossing the glowing surface.

But there was another development of the science of the Crystal Cities which interested them far more than this—for after all they could not only see the Worlds of Space for themselves, but circumnavigate them if they chose.

During their stay they were shown on these same screens the pictorial history of the world whose guests they were. These pictures, which they recognised as an immeasurable development of what is called the cinematographic process on Earth, extended through the whole gamut of the satellite's life. They formed, in fact, the means by which the children of Ganymede were taught the history of their world.

It was, of course, inevitable that the *Astronef* should prove an object of intense interest to their hosts. They had solved the problem of the Resolution of Forces, as Professor Rennick had done, and, as they were shown pictorially, a vessel had been made which embodied the principles of attraction and repulsion. It had risen from the surface of Ganymede, and then, possibly because its engines could not develop sufficient repulsive force, the tremendous pull of the giant planet had dragged it away. It had vanished through the cloud-belts towards the flaming surface beneath—and the experiment had never been repeated.

Here, however, was a vessel which had actually, as Redgrave had convinced his hosts by means of celestial maps and drawings of his own, left a planet close to the Sun, and safely crossed the tremendous gulf of six hundred and fifty million miles which separated Jupiter from the centre of the system. Moreover he had twice proved her powers by taking his host and two of his newly-made friends, the chief astronomers of Ganymede, on a short trip across Space to Calisto and Europa, the second satellite of Jupiter, which, to their very grave interest, they found had already passed the stage in which Ganymede was, and had lapsed into the icy silence of death.

It was these two journeys which led to the last adventure of the *Astronef* in the Jovian System. Both Redgrave and Zaidie had determined, at whatever risk, to pass through the cloud-belts of Jupiter, and catch a glimpse, if only a glimpse, of a world in the making. Their host and the two astronomers, after a certain amount of quiet discussion, accepted their invitation to accompany them, and on the morning of the eighth day after their landing on Ganymede, the *Astronef* rose from the plain outside the Crystal City, and directed her course towards the centre of the vast disc of Jupiter.

She was followed by the telescopes of all the observatories until she vanished through the brilliant cloud-band, eighty-five thousand miles long and some five thousand miles broad, which stretched from east to west of the planet. At the same moment the voyagers lost sight of Ganymede and his sister satellites.

The temperature of the interior of the *Astronef* began to rise as soon as the upper cloud-belt was passed. Under this, spread out a vast field of brown-red cloud, rent here and there into holes and gaps like those storm-cavities in the atmosphere of the Sun, which are commonly known as sun-spots. This lower stratum of cloud appeared to be the scene of terrific storms, compared with which the fiercest earthly tempests were mere zephyrs.

After falling some five hundred miles further they found themselves surrounded by what seemed an ocean of fire, but still the internal temperature had only risen from seventy to ninety-five. The engines were well under control. Only about a fourth of the total R. Force was being developed, and the *Astronef* was dropping swiftly, but steadily.

Redgrave, who was in the conning-tower controlling the engines, beckoned to Zaidie and said:

"Shall we go on?"

"Yes," she said." Now we've got as far as this I want to see what Jupiter is like, and where you are not afraid to go, I'll go."

"If I'm afraid at all it's only because you are with me, Zaidie," he replied, "but I've only got a fourth of the power turned on yet, so there's plenty of margin."

The *Astronef*, therefore, continued to sink through what seemed to be a fathomless ocean of whirling, blazing clouds, and the internal temperature went on rising slowly but steadily. Their guests, without showing the slightest sign of any emotion, walked about the upper deck now singly and now together, apparently absorbed by the strange scene about them.

At length, after they had been dropping for some five hours by *Astronef* time, one of them, uttering a sharp exclamation, pointed to an enormous rift about fifty miles away. A dull, red glare was streaming up out of it. The next moment the brown cloud-floor beneath them seemed to split up into enormous wreaths of vapour, which whirled up on all sides of them, and a few minutes later they caught their first glimpse of the true surface of Jupiter.

It lay as nearly as they could judge, some two thousand miles beneath them, a distance which the telescopes reduced to less than twenty; and they saw for a few moments the world that was in the making. Through floating seas of misty steam they beheld what seemed to them to be vast continents shape themselves and melt away into oceans of flames. Whole mountain ranges of glowing lava were hurled up miles high to take shape for an instant and then fall away again, leaving fathomless gulfs of fiery mist in their place.

Then waves of molten matter rose up again out of the gulfs, tens of miles high and hundreds of miles long, surged forward, and met with a concussion like that of millions of earthly thunder-clouds. Minute after minute they remained writhing and struggling with each other, flinging up spurts of flaming matter far above their crests. Other waves followed them, climbing up their bases as a sea-surge runs up the side of a smooth, slanting rock. Then from the midst of them a jet of living fire leapt up hundreds of miles into the lurid atmosphere above, and then, with a crash and a roar which shook the vast Jovian firmament, the battling lava-waves would split apart and sink down into the all-surrounding fire-ocean, like two grappling giants who had strangled each other in their final struggle.

"It's just Hell let loose!" said Murgatroyd to himself as he looked down upon the terrific scene through one of the portholes of the engine-room; "and, with all respect to my lord and her ladyship, those that come this near almost deserve to stop in it."

Meanwhile, Redgrave and Zaidie and their three guests were so absorbed in the tremendous spectacle, that for a few moments no one noticed that they were dropping faster and faster towards the world which Murgatroyd, according to his lights, had not inaptly described. As for Zaidie, all her fears were for the time being lost in wonder, until she saw her husband take a swift glance round upwards and downwards, and then go up into the conning-tower. She followed him quickly, and said:

"What is the matter, Lenox, are we falling too quickly?"

"Much faster than we should," he replied, sending a signal to Murgatroyd to increase the force by three-tenths.

The answering signal came back, but still the *Astronef* continued to fall with terrific rapidity, and the awful landscape beneath them—a landscape of fire and chaos—broadened out and became more and more distinct.

He sent two more signals down in quick succession. Three-fourths of the whole repulsive power of the engines was now being exerted—a force which would have been sufficient to hurl the *Astronef* up from the surface of the Earth like a feather in a whirlwind. Her downward course became a little slower, but still she did not stop. Zaidie, white to the lips, looked down upon the hideous scene beneath and slipped her hand through Redgrave's arm. He looked at her for an instant and then turned his head away with a jerk, and sent down the last signal.

The whole energy of the engines was now directing the maximum of the R. Force against the surface of Jupiter, but still, as every moment passed in a speechless agony of apprehension, it grew nearer and nearer. The fire-waves mounted higher and higher, the roar of the fiery surges grew louder and louder. Then in a momentary lull, he put his arm round her, drew her close up to him, and kissed her and said:

"That's all we can do, dear. We've come too close and he's too strong for us."

She returned his kiss and said quite steadily:

"Well, at any rate, I'm with you, and it won't last long, will it?"

"Not very long now, I'm afraid," he said between his clenched teeth. And then he pulled her close to him again, and together they looked down into the storm-tossed hell towards which they were falling at the rate of nearly a hundred miles a minute.

Almost the next moment they felt a little jerk beneath their feet—a jerk upwards; and Redgrave shook himself out of the half stupor into which he was falling and said:

"Hallo, what's that! I believe we're stopping—yes, we are—and we're beginning to rise, too. Look, dear, the clouds are coming down upon us—fast too! I wonder what sort of miracle that is. Ay, what's the matter, little woman?"

Zaidie's head had dropped heavily on his shoulder. A glance showed him that she had fainted. He could do nothing more in the conning-tower, so he picked her up and carried her towards the companion-way, past his three guests, who were standing in the middle of the upper deck round a table on which lay a large sheet of paper.

He took her below and laid her on her bed, and in a few minutes he had brought her to and told her that it was all right. Then he gave her a drink of brandy-and-water, and went back on to the upper deck. As he reached the top of the stairway one of the astronomers came towards him with the sheet of paper in his hand, smiling gravely, and pointing to a sketch upon it.

He took the paper under one of the electric lights and looked at it. The sketch was a plan of the Jovian System. There were some signs written along one side, which he did not understand, but he divined that they were calculations. Still, there was no mistaking the diagram. There was a circle representing the huge bulk of Jupiter; there were four smaller circles at varying distances in a nearly straight line from it, and between the nearest of these and the planet was the figure of the *Astronef*, with an arrow pointing upwards.

"Ah, I see!" he said, forgetting for a moment that the other did not understand him, "That was the miracle! The four satellites came into line with us just as the pull of Jupiter was getting too much for our engines, and their combined pull just turned the scale. Well, thank God for that, sir, for in a few minutes more we should have been cinders!"

The astronomer smiled again as he took the paper back. Meanwhile the *Astronef* was rushing upward like a meteor through the clouds. In ten minutes the limits of the Jovian atmosphere were passed. Stars and suns and planets blazed out of the black vault of Space, and the great disc of the World that Is to Be once more covered the floor of Space beneath them—an ocean of cloud, covering continents of lava and seas of flame.

They passed Io and Europa, which changed from new to full moons as they sped by towards the Sun, and then the golden yellow crescent of Ganymede also began to fill out to the half and full disc, and by the tenth hour of earth-time after they had risen from its surface, the *Astronef* was once more lying beside the gate of the Crystal City.

At midnight on the second night after their return, the ringed shape of Saturn, attended by his eight satellites, hung in the zenith magnificently inviting. The *Astronef*'s engines had been replenished after the exhaustion of their struggle with the might of Jupiter. They said farewell to their friends of the dying world. The doors of the air chamber closed. The signal tinkled in the engine-room, and a few moments later a blur of white lights on the brown background of the surrounding desert was all they could distinguish of the Crystal City under whose domes they had seen and learnt so much.

CHAPTER 17

THE RELATIVE POSITION of the two giants of the Solar System at the moment when the *Astronef* left the surface of Ganymede, was such that she had to make a journey of rather more than 340,000,000 miles before she passed within the confines of the Saturnine System.

At first her speed, as shown by the observations which Redgrave took by means of instruments designed for such a voyage by Professor Rennick, was comparatively slow. This was due to the tremendous pull of Jupiter and its four moons on the fabric of the vessel. The backward drag rapidly decreased as the pull of Saturn and his System began to overmaster that of Jupiter.

It so happened, too, that Uranus, the next outer planet of the Solar System, 1,700,000,000 miles away from the Sun, was approaching its conjunction with Saturn, and so assisted in producing a constant acceleration of speed.

Jupiter and his satellites dropped behind, sinking, as it seemed to the wanderers, down into the bottomless gulf of Space, but still forming by far the most brilliant and splendid object in the skies. The far-distant Sun which, seen from the Saturnian System, has only about a ninetieth of the superficial extent which he presents to the Earth, dwindled away rapidly until it began to look like a huge planet, with the Earth, Venus, Mars, and Mercury as satellites. Beyond the orbit of Saturn, Uranus, with his eight moons, was shining with the lustre of a star of the first magnitude, and far above and beyond him again hung the pale disc of Neptune, the Outer Guard of the Solar System, separated from the Sun by a gulf of more than 2,750,000,000 miles.

When two-thirds of the distance between Jupiter and Saturn had been traversed, Ringed Orb lay beneath them like a vast globe surrounded by an enormous circular ocean of many-coloured fire, divided, as it were, by circular shores of shade and darkness. On the side opposite to them a gigantic conical shadow extended beyond the confines of the ocean of light. It was the shadow of half the globe of Saturn cast by the Sun across his rings. Three little dark spots were also travelling across the surface of the rings. They were the shadows of Mimas, Encealadus, and Tethys, the three inner satellites. Japetus, the most distant, which revolves at a distance ten times greater than that of the Moon from the Earth, was rising to their left above the edge of the rings, a pale, yellow, little disc shining feebly against the black background of Space. The rest of the eight satellites were hidden behind the enormous bulk of the planet, and the infinitely vaster area of the rings.

Day after day Zaidie and her husband had been exhausting the possibilities of the English language in attempting to describe to each other the multiplying marvels of the wondrous scene which they were approaching at a speed of more than a hundred miles a second, and at length Zaidie, after nearly an hour's absolute silence, during which they sat with eyes fastened to their telescopes, looked up and said:

"It's no use, Lenox, all the fine words that we've been trying to think of have just been wasted. The angels may have a language that you could describe that in, but we haven't. If it wouldn't be something like blasphemy I should drop down to the commonplace, and call Saturn a celestial spinning-top, with bands of light and shadow instead of colours all round it."

"Not at all a bad simile either," laughed Redgrave, as he got up from his chair with a yawn and a stretch of his athletic limbs, "still, it's as well that you said celestial, for, after all, that's about the best word we've found yet. Certainly the ringed world is the most nearly heavenly thing we've seen so far."

"But," he went on, "I think it's about time we were stopping this headlong fall of ours. Do you see how the landscape is spreading out round us? That means that we're dropping pretty fast. Whereabouts would you like to land? At present we're heading straight for Saturn's north pole."

"I think I'd rather see what the rings are like first," said Zaidie; "couldn't we go across them?"

"Certainly we can," he replied, "only we'll have to be a bit careful."

"Careful, what of—collisions? I suppose you're thinking of Proctor's explanation that the rings are formed of multitudes of tiny satellites?"

"Yes, but I should go a little farther than that, I should say that his rings and his eight satellites are to Saturn what the planets generally and the ring of the Asteroides are to the Sun, and if that is the case—I mean if we find the rings made up of myriads of tiny bodies flying round with Saturn—it might get a bit risky.

"You see the outside ring is a bit over 160,000 miles across, and it revolves in less than eleven hours. In other words we might find the ring a sort of celestial maelstrom, and if we once got into the whirl, and Saturn exerted his full pull on us, we might become a satellite, too, and go on swinging round with the rest for a good bit of eternity."

"Very well, then," she said, "of course we don't want to do anything of that sort, but there's something else I think we could do," she went on, taking up a copy of Proctor's "Saturn and its System," which she had been reading just after breakfast. "You see those rings are, all together, about 10,000 miles broad; there's a gap of about 1700 miles between the big dark one and the middle bright one, and it's nearly 10,000 miles from the edge of the bright ring to the surface of Saturn. Now why shouldn't we get in between the inner ring and the planet? If Proctor was right and the rings are made of tiny satellites and there are myriads of them, of course they'll pull up while Saturn pulls down. In fact Flammarion says somewhere, that along Saturn's equator there is no weight at all."

"Quite possible," said Redgrave, "and, if you like, we'll go and prove it. Of course, if the *Astronef* weighs absolutely nothing between Saturn and the rings, we can easily get away. The only thing that I object to is getting into this 170,000 mile vortex, being whizzed round with Saturn every ten and a half hours, and sauntering round the Sun at 21,000 miles an hour."

"Don't!" she said, "really it isn't good to think about these things, situated as we are. Fancy, in a single year of Saturn there are nearly 25,000 days. Why, we should each of us be about thirty years older when we got round, even if we lived, which, of course, we shouldn't. By the way, how long could we live for, if the worst came to the worst?"

"Given water, about one earth-year at the outside," he replied, "but, of course, we shall be home long before that."

"If we don't become one of the satellites of Saturn," she replied, "or get dragged away by something into the outer depths of Space."

Meanwhile the downward speed of the *Astronef* had been considerably checked. The vast circle of the rings seemed to suddenly expand, and soon it covered the whole floor of the vault of Space.

As the *Astronef* dropped towards what might be called the limit of the northern tropic of Saturn, the spectacle presented by the rings became every minute more and more marvellous—purple and silver, black and gold, dotted with myriads of brilliant points of many-coloured lights, they stretched upwards like vast rainbows into the Saturnian sky as the *Astronef*'s position changed with regard to the horizon of the planet. The nearer they approached the surface, the nearer the gigantic arch of the many coloured rings approached the zenith. Sun and stars sank down behind it, for now they were dropping through the fifteen-year-long twilight that reigns over that portion of the globe of Saturn which, during half of his year of thirty terrestrial years, is turned away from the Sun.

The further they dropped towards the rings the more certain it became that the theory of the great English astronomer was the correct one. Seen through the telescopes at a distance of only thirty or forty thousand miles, it became perfectly plain that the outer or darker ring as seen from the Earth was composed of myriads of tiny bodies so far separated from each other that the rayless blackness of Space could be seen through them.

"It's quite evident," said Redgrave, "that those are rings of what we should call meteorites on earth, atoms of matter which Saturn threw off into Space after the satellites were formed."

"And I shouldn't wonder, if you will excuse my interrupting you," said Zaidie, "if the moons themselves have been made up of a lot of these things going together when they were only gas, or nebula, or something of that sort. In fact, when Saturn was a good deal younger than he is now, he may have had a lot more rings and no moons, and now these aerolites, or whatever they are, can't come together and make moons, because they've got too solid."

Meanwhile the *Astronef* was rapidly approaching that portion of Saturn's surface which was illuminated by the rays of the Sun, streaming under the lower arch of the inner ring.

As they passed under it the whole scene suddenly changed. The rings vanished. Overhead was an arch of brilliant light a hundred miles thick, spanning the whole of the visible heavens. Below lay the sunlit surface of Saturn divided into light and dark bands of enormous breadth.

The band immediately below them was of a brilliant silver-grey, very much like the central zone of Jupiter. North of this on the one side stretched the long shadow of the rings, and southward other bands of alternating white and gold and deep purple succeeded each other till they were lost in the curvature of the vast planet. The poles were of course invisible since the *Astronef* was now too near to the surface; but on their approach they had seen unmistakable evidence of snow and ice.

As soon as they were exactly under the Ring-arch, Redgrave shut off the R. Force, and, somewhat to their astonishment, the *Astronef* began to revolve slowly on its axis, giving them the idea that the Saturnian System was revolving round them. The arch seemed to sink beneath their feet while the belts of the planet rose above them.

"What on earth is the matter?" said Zaidie. "Everything has gone upside down."

"Which shows." replied Redgrave, "that as soon as the *Astronef* became neutral the rings pulled harder than the planet, I suppose because we're so near to them, and, instead of falling on to Saturn, we shall have to push up at him."

"Oh yes, I see that," said Zaidie, "but after all it does look a little bit bewildering, doesn't it, to be on your feet one minute and on your head the next?"

"It is, rather; but you ought to be getting accustomed to that sort of thing now. In a few minutes neither you, nor I, nor anything else will have any weight. We shall be just between the attraction of the Rings and Saturn, so you'd better go and sit down, for if you were to give a bit of an extra spring in walking you might be knocking that pretty head of yours against the roof," said Redgrave, as he went to turn the R. Force on to the edge of the Rings.

A vast sea of silver cloud seemed now to descend upon them. Then they entered it, and for nearly half-an-hour the *Astronef* was totally enveloped in a sea of pearl-grey luminous mist.

"Atmosphere!" said Redgrave, as he went to the conning-tower and signalled to Murgatroyd to start the propellers. They continued to rise and the mist began to drift past them in patches, showing that the propellers were driving them ahead.

They now rose swiftly towards the surface of the planet. The cloud wrack got thinner and thinner, and presently they found themselves floating in a clear atmosphere between two seas of cloud, the one above them being much less dense than the one below.

"I believe we shall see Saturn on the other side of that,' said Zaidie, looking up at it. "Oh dear, there we are going round again."

"Reaching the point of neutral attraction," said Redgrave; "once more you'd better sit down in case of accidents."

Instead of dropping into her deck chair as she would have done on Earth, she took hold of the arms and pulled herself into it, saying:

"Really it seems rather absurd to have to do this sort of thing. Fancy having to hold yourself into a chair. I suppose I hardly weigh anything at all now"

"Not much," said Redgrave, stooping down and taking hold of the end of the chair with both hands. Without any apparent effort he raised her about five feet from the floor, and held her there while

the *Astronef* made another revolution. For a moment he let go, and she and the chair floated between the roof and the floor of the deck-chamber. Then he pulled the chair away from under her, and as the floor of the vessel once more turned towards Saturn, he took hold of her hands and brought her to her feet on deck again.

"I ought to have had a photograph of you like that!" he laughed. "I wonder what they'd think of it at home?"

"If you had taken one I should certainly have broken the negative. The very idea—a photograph of me standing on nothing! Besides, they'd never believe it on Earth."

"We might have got old Andrew to make an affidavit to that effect," he began.

"Don't talk nonsense, Lenox! Look! There's something much more interesting. There's Saturn at last. Now I wonder if we shall find any sort of life there—and shall we be able to breathe the air?"

"I hardly think so," he said, as the *Astronef* dropped slowly through the thin cloud-veil. "You know spectrum analysis has proved that there is a gas in Saturn's atmosphere which we know nothing about, and, however good it may be for the Saturnians, it's not very likely that it would agree with us, so I think we'd better be content with our own. Besides, the atmosphere is so enormously dense that even if we could breathe it it might squash us up. You see we're only accustomed to fifteen pounds on the square inch, and it may be hundreds of pounds here."

"Well," said Zaidie, "I haven't got any particular desire to be flattened out like that, or squeezed dry like an orange. It's not at all a nice idea, is it? But, look, Lenox," she went on, pointing downwards, "surely this isn't air at all, or at least it's something between air and water. Aren't these things swimming about in it—something like fish in the sea? They can't be clouds, and they aren't either fish or birds. They don't fly or float. Well, this is certainly more wonderful than anything else we've seen, though it doesn't look very pleasant. They're not nice looking, are they? I wonder if they are at all dangerous!"

While she was saying this Zaidie had gone to her telescope, and was sweeping the surface of Saturn, which was now about a hundred miles distant. Her husband was doing the same. In fact, for the time being they were all eyes, for they were looking on a stranger sight than man or woman had ever seen before.

Underneath the inner cloud-veil the atmosphere of Saturn appeared to them somewhat as the lower depths of the ocean would appear to a diver, granted that he was able to see for hundreds of miles about him. Its colour was a pale greenish yellow. The outside thermometers showed that the temperature was a hundred and seventy-five. In fact, the interior of the *Astronef* was getting uncomfortably like a Turkish bath, and Redgrave took the opportunity of at once freshening and cooling the air by releasing a little oxygen from the cylinders.

From what they could see of the surface of Saturn it seemed to be a dead level, greyish-brown in colour, and not divided into oceans and continents. In fact there were no signs whatever of water within range of their telescopes. There was nothing that looked like cities, or any human habitations, but the ground, as they got nearer to it, seemed to be covered with a very dense vegetable growth, not unlike gigantic forms of seaweed, and of somewhat the same colour. In fact, as Zaidie remarked, the surface of Saturn was not at all unlike what the floors of the ocean of the Earth might be if they were laid bare.

It was evident that the life of this portion of Saturn was not what, for want of a more exact word, might be called terrestrial. Its inhabitants, however they were constituted, floated about in the depths of this semi-gaseous ocean as the denizens of earthly seas did in the terrestrial oceans. Already their telescopes enabled them to make out enormous moving shapes, black and grey-brown and pale red, swimming about, evidently by their own volition, rising and falling and often sinking down on to the gigantic vegetation which covered the surface, possibly for the purpose of feeding. But it was also evident that they resembled the inhabitants of earthly oceans in another respect, since it was easy to see that they preyed upon each other.

"I don't like the look of those creatures at all," said Zaidie, when the *Astronef* had come to a stop and was floating about five miles above the surface. "They're altogether too uncanny. They look to me something like jelly-fish about the size of whales, only they have eyes and mouths. Did you ever see such awful looking eyes, bigger than soup-plates and as bright as a cat's. I suppose that's because of the dim light. And the nasty wormy sort of way they swim, or fly, or whatever it is. Lenox, I don't know what the rest of Saturn may be like, but I certainly don't like this part. It's quite too creepy and unearthly for my taste. Look at the horrors fighting and eating each other. That's the only bit of earthly character they've got about them; the big ones eating the little ones. I hope they won't take the *Astronef* for something nice to eat."

"They'd find her a pretty tough morsel if they did," laughed Redgrave, "but still we may as well get some steering way on her in case of accident."

CHAPTER 18

A FEW MOMENTS LATER he sent a signal to Murgatroyd in the engine-room. The propellers began to revolve slowly, beating the dense air and driving the Star Navigator at a speed of about twenty miles an hour through the depths of this strangely-peopled ocean.

They approached nearer and nearer to the surface, and as they did so the strange creatures about them grew more and more numerous. They were certainly the most extraordinary living things that human eyes had ever looked upon. Zaidie's comparison to the whale and the jelly-fish was by no means incorrect; only when they got near enough to them they found, to their astonishment, that they were double-headed—that is to say, they had a head furnished with mouth, nostrils, ear-holes, and eyes at each end of their bodies.

The larger of the creatures appeared to have a certain amount of respect for each other. Now and then they witnessed a battle-royal between two of the monsters who were pursuing the same prey. Their method of attack was as follows: The assailant would rise above his opponent or prey, and then, dropping on to its back, envelop it and begin tearing at its sides and under parts with huge beak-like jaws, somewhat resembling those of the largest kind of the earthly octopus, only infinitely more formidable. The substance composing their bodies appeared to be not unlike that of a terrestrial jelly-fish, but much denser. It seemed from their motions to have the tenacity of soft India rubber save at the headed ends, where it was much harder. The necks were protected for about fifty feet by huge scales of a dull, greenish hue.

When one of them had overpowered an enemy or a victim the two sank down into the vegetation, and the victor began to eat the vanquished. Their means of locomotion consisted of huge fins, or rather half fins, half wings, of which they had three laterally arranged behind each head, and four much longer and narrower, above and below, which seemed to be used mainly for steering purposes.

They moved with equal ease in either direction, and they appeared to rise or fall by inflating or deflating the middle portions of their bodies, somewhat as fish do with their swimming bladders.

The light in the lower regions of this strange ocean was dimmer than earthly twilight, although the *Astronef* was steadily making her way beneath the arch of the rings towards the sunlit hemisphere.

"I wonder what the effect of the searchlight would be on these fellows!" said Redgrave. "Those huge eyes of theirs are evidently only suited to dim light. Let's try and dazzle some of them."

"I hope it won't be a case of the moths and the candle!" said Zaidie. "They don't seem to have taken much interest in us so far. Perhaps they haven't been able to see properly, but suppose they were attracted by the light and began crowding round us and fastening on to us, as the horrible things do with each other. What should we do then? They might drag us down and perhaps keep us there; but there's one thing, they'd never eat us, because we could keep closed up and die respectably together."

"Not much fear of that, little woman," he said, "we're too strong for them. Hardened steel and toughened glass ought to be more than a match for a lot of exaggerated jelly-fish like these," said Redgrave, as he switched on the head search-light. "We've come here to see strange things and we may as well see them. Ah, would you, my friend. No, this is not one of your sort, and it isn't meant to eat."

An enormous double-headed monster, apparently some four hundred feet long, came floating towards them as the search-light flashed out, and others began instantly to crowd about them, just as Zaidie had feared.

"Lenox, for Heaven's sake be careful!" cried Zaidie, shrinking up beside him as the huge, hideous head, with its saucer eyes and enormous beak-like jaws wide open, came towards them. "And look, there are more coming. Can't we go up and get away from them?"

"Wait a minute, little woman," replied Redgrave, who was beginning to feel the passion of adventure thrilling in his nerves "If we fought the Martian air fleet and licked it I think we can manage these things. Let's see how he likes the light."

As he spoke he flashed the full glare of the five thousand candle-power lamp full on to the creature's great cat-like eyes.

Instantly it bent itself up into an arc. The two heads, each the exact image of the other, came together. The four eyes glared half dazzled into the conning-tower and the four huge jaws snapped viciously together.

"Lenox, Lenox, for goodness sake let us go up!" cried Zaidie shrinking still closer to him. "That thing's too horrible to look at."

"It is a beast, isn't it?" he said, "but I think we can cut him in two without much trouble."

He signalled for full speed. The *Astronef* ought to have sprung forward and driven her ram through the huge, brick-red body of the hideous creature which was now only a couple of hundred yards from them; but instead of that a slow, jarring, grinding thrill seemed to run through her, and she stopped. The next moment Murgatroyd put his head up through the companion-way which led from the upper deck to the conning-tower, and said in a tone whose calm indicated, as usual, resignation to the worst that could happen:

"My lord, two of those beasts, fishes or live balloons, or whatever they are, have come across the propellers. They're cut up a good bit, but I've had to stop the engines, and they're clinging all round the after part. We're going down, too. Shall I disconnect the propellers and turn on the repulsion?"

"Yes, certainly, Andrew!" cried Zaidie, "and all of it, too. Look, Lenox, that horrible thing is coming. Suppose it broke the glass, and we couldn't breathe this atmosphere!"

As she spoke the enormous, double-headed body advanced until it completely enveloped the forward part of the *Astronef.* The two hideous heads came close to the sides of the conning-tower; the huge, palely luminous eyes looked in upon them. Zaidie, in her terror, even thought that she saw something like human curiosity in them.

Then, as Murgatroyd disappeared to obey the orders which Redgrave had sanctioned with a quick nod, the heads approached still closer, and she heard the ends of the pointed jaws, which she now saw were armed with shark-like teeth, striking against the thick glass walls of the conning-tower.

"Don't be frightened, dear!" he said, putting his arm round her, just as he had done when they thought they were falling into the fiery seas of Jupiter. "You'll see something happen to this gentleman soon. Big and all as he is there won't be much left of him in a few minutes. They are like those monsters they found in the lowest depths of our own seas. They can only live under tremendous pressure. That's why we didn't find any of them up above. This chap'll burst like a bubble presently. Meanwhile, there's no use in stopping here. Suppose you go below and brew some coffee and bring it up on deck, while I go and see how things are looking aft. It doesn't do you any good, you know, to be looking at monsters of this sort. You can see what's left of them later on. You might bring the cognac decanter up too."

Zaidie was not at all sorry to obey him, for the horrible sight had almost sickened her.

They were still under the arch of the rings, and so, when the full strength of the R. Force was directed against the body of Saturn, the vessel sprang upwards like a projectile fired from a cannon.

Redgrave went back into the conning-tower to see what happened to their assailant. It was already trying vainly to detach itself and sink back into a more congenial element. As the pressure of the atmosphere decreased its huge body swelled up into still huger proportions. The skin on the two heads puffed up as though air was being pumped in under it. The great eyes protruded out of their sockets; the jaws opened widely as though the creature were gasping for breath.

Meanwhile Murgatroyd was seeing something very similar at the after end, and wondering what was going to happen to his propellers, the blades of which were deeply imbedded in the jelly-like flesh of the monsters.

The *Astronef* leaped higher and higher, and the hideous bodies which were clinging to her swelled out huger and huger, and Redgrave even fancied that he heard something like cries of pain from both heads on either side of the conning-tower. They passed through the inner cloud-veil, and then the *Astronef* began to turn on her axis, and, just as the outer envelope came into view the enormously distended bulk of the monsters collapsed, and their fragments, seeming now more like the tatters of a burst balloon than portions of a once-living creature, dropped from the body of the *Astronef* and floated away down into what had once been their native element.

"Difference of environment means a lot, after all," said Redgrave to himself. "I should have called that either a lie or a miracle if I hadn't seen it, and I'm jolly glad I sent Zaidie down below."

"Here's your coffee, Lenox," said her voice from the upper deck the next moment, "only it doesn't seem to want to stop in the cups, and the cups keep getting off the saucers. I suppose we're turning upside down again."

Redgrave stepped somewhat gingerly on to the deck, for his body had so little weight under the double attraction of Saturn and the Rings that a very slight effort would have sent him flying up to the roof of the deck-chamber.

"That's exactly as you please," he said, "just hold that table steady a minute. We shall have our centre of gravity back soon. And now, as to the main question, suppose we take a trip across the sunlit hemisphere of Saturn to, what I suppose we should call, on Earth, the South Pole. We can get resistance from the Rings, and as we are here we may as well see what the rest of Saturn is like. You see, if our theory is correct as to the Rings gathering up most of the atmosphere of Saturn about its equator, we shall get to higher altitudes where the air is thinner and more like our own, and therefore it s quite possible that we shall find different forms of life in it too—or if you've had enough of Saturn and would prefer a trip to Uranus—?"

"No, thanks," said Zaidie quickly. "To tell you the truth, Lenox, I've had almost enough star-wandering for one honeymoon, and though we've seen nice things as well as horrible things—especially those ghastly, slimy creatures down there—I'm beginning to feel a bit homesick for good old mother Earth. You see, we're nearly a thousand million miles from home, and, even with you, it makes one feel a bit lonely. I vote we explore the rest of this hemisphere up to the pole, and then, as they say at sea—I mean our sea—'bout ship, and see if we can find our own old world again. After all, it's more homelike than any of these, isn't it?"

"Just take your telescope and look at it," said Redgrave, pointing towards the Sun, with its little cluster of attendant planets. "It looks something like one of Jupiter's little moons down there, doesn't it, only not quite as big?"

"Yes, it does, but that doesn't matter. The fact is that it's there, and we know what it's like, and it's home, if it is a thousand million miles away, and that's everything."

By this time they had passed through the outer band of clouds. The vast, sunlit arch of the Rings towered up to the zenith, apparently spanning the whole visible heavens. Below and in front of them lay the enormous semi-circle of the hemisphere which was turned towards the Sun, shrouded by its many coloured bands of clouds. The R. Force was directed strongly against the lower Ring, and the Asfronef dropped rapidly in a slanting direction through the cloud-bands towards the southern temperate zone of the planet.

They passed through the second, or dark, cloud-band at the rate of about three thousand miles an hour, aided by the Repulsion against the Rings and the attraction of the planet, and soon after lunch, the materials of which now consented to remain on the table, they passed through the clouds and found themselves in a new world of wonders.

On a far vaster scale, it was the Earth during that period of its development which is called the Reptilian Age. The atmosphere was still dense and loaded with aqueous vapour, but the waters had already been divided from the land.

They passed over vast, marshy continents and islands, and warm seas, above which thin clouds of steam still hung, and as they swept southward with the propellers working at their utmost speed, they caught glimpses of giant forms rising out of the steamy waters near the land; of others crawling slowly over it, dragging their huge bulk through a tremendous vegetation, which they crushed down as they passed, as a sheep on earth might push its way through a field of standing corn.

Other and even stranger shapes, broad-winged and ungainly, fluttered with a slow, bat-like motion through the lower strata of the atmosphere.

Every now and then during the voyage across the temperate zone the propellers were slowed down to enable them to witness some Titanic conflict between the gigantic denizens of land and sea and air. But Zaidie had had enough of horrors on the Saturnian equator, and so she was quite content to watch this phase of evolution working itself out (as it had happened on the Earth many thousands of ages ago) from a convenient distance. Wherefore the *Astronef* sped on southward without approaching the surface nearer than a couple of miles.

"It'll be all very nice to see and remember and dream about afterwards," she said, "but really I don't think I can stand any more monsters just now, at least not at close quarters, and I'm quite sure if those things can live there we couldn't, any more than we could have lived on Earth a million years or so ago. No, really I don't want to land, Lenox; let's go on."

They went on at a speed of about a hundred miles an hour, and, as they progressed southward, both the atmosphere and the landscape rapidly changed. The air grew clearer and the clouds lighter. Lands and seas were more sharply divided, and both teeming with life. The seas still swarmed with serpentine monsters of the saurian type, and the firmer lands were peopled by huge animals, mastodons, bears, giant tapirs, myledons, deinotheriums, and a score of other species too strange for them to recognise by any earthly likeness, which roamed in great herds through the vast twilit forests and over boundless plains covered with grey-blue vegetation.

Here, too, they found mountains for the first time on Saturn; mountains steep-sided, and many earth-miles high.

As the *Astronef* was skirting the side of one of these ranges Redgrave allowed it to approach more closely than he had so far done to the surface of Saturn.

"I shouldn't wonder if we found some of the higher forms of life up here," he said. "If there is anything here that's going to develop some clay into the human race of Saturn it would naturally get up here."

"I should hope so," said Zaidie, "and just as far as possible out of the reach of those unutterable horrors on the equator. That would be one of the first signs they would show of superior intelligence. Look, I believe there are some of them. Do you see those holes in the mountain side there? And there they are, something like gorillas, only twice as big, and up the trees, too—and what trees! They must be seven or eight hundred feet high."

"Tree and cave-dwellers, and ancestors of the future royal race of Saturn, I suppose!" said Redgrave. "They don't look very nice, do they? Still, there's no doubt about their being far superior in intelligence to what we left behind us. Evidently this atmosphere is too thin for the two-headed jelly-fishes and the saurians to breathe. These creatures have found that out in a few hundreds of generations, and so they have come to live up here out of the way. Vegetarians, I suppose, or perhaps they live on smaller monkeys and other animals, just as our ancestors did."

"Really, Lenox," said Zaidie, turning round and facing him, "I must say that you have a most unpleasant way of alluding to one's ancestors. They couldn't help what they were."

"Well, dear," he said, going towards her, "marvellous as the

Stanley L Wood

miracle seems, I'm heretic enough to believe it possible that your ancestors even, millions of years ago, perhaps, may have been something like those; but then, of course, you know I'm a hopeless Darwinian."

"And, therefore, entirely horrid, as I've often said before when you get on subjects like these. Not, of course, that I'm ashamed of my poor relations; and then, after all, your Darwin was quite wrong when he talked about the descent of man—and woman. We—especially the women—have ascended from that sort of thing, if there's any truth in the story at all; though, personally, I must say I prefer dear old Mother Eve."

"Who never had a sweeter daughter than—!" he replied, drawing her towards him.

"Very prettily put, my Lord," she laughed, releasing herself with a gentle twirl; and now I'll go and get dinner ready," she said. "After all, it doesn't matter what world one's in, one gets hungry all the same."

The dinner, which was eaten somewhere in the middle of the fifteen-year-long day of Saturn, was a very pleasant one, because they were now nearing the turning-point of their trip into the depths of Space, and thoughts of home and friends were already beginning to fly back across the thousand-million-mile gulf which lay between them and the Earth which they had left only a little more than two months ago.

While they were at dinner the *Astronef* rose above the mountains and resumed her southward course. Zaidie brought the coffee up on deck as usual after dinner, and, while Redgrave smoked his cigar and Zaidie her cigarette, they luxuriated in the magnificent spectacle of the sunlit side of Rings towering up, rainbow built on rainbow, to the zenith of their visible heavens.

"What a pity there aren't any words to describe it!" said Zaidie. "I wonder if the descendants of the ancestors of the future human race on Saturn will invent anything like a suitable language. I wonder how they'll talk about those Rings millions of years hence."

"By that time there may not be any Rings," Lenox replied, blowing a ring of smoke from his own lips. "Look at that—made in a moment and gone in a moment—and yet on exactly the same principle, it gives one a dim idea of the difference between time and eternity. After all it's only another example of Kelvin's theory of vortices. Nebulae, and asteroids, and planet-rings, and smoke-rings are really all made on the same principle."

"My dear Lenox, if you're going to get as philosophical and as commonplace as that I'm going to bed. Now that I come to think of it, I've been about fifteen earth-hours out of bed, so it's about time I went. It's your turn to make the coffee in the morning—our morning I mean—and you'll wake me in time to see the South Pole of Saturn, won't you? You're not coming yet, I suppose?"

"Not just yet, dear. I want to see a bit more of this, and then I must go through the engines and see that they're all right and ready for that thousand million mile homeward voyage you're talking about. You can have a good ten hours' sleep without missing much, I think, for there doesn't seem to be anything more interesting than our own Arctic life down there. So good-night, little woman, don't have too many nightmares."

"Good-night!" she said, "if you hear me shout you'll know that you've to come and protect me from monsters. Weren't those two-headed brutes just too horrid for words? Good-night, dear!"

CHAPTER 19

A LITTLE BEFORE SIX (Earth time) on the fourth morning after they had cleared the confines of the Saturnian System, Redgrave went as usual into the conning-tower to examine the instruments and to see that everything was in order. To his intense surprise he found, on looking at the gravitational compass, which was to the *Astronef* what the ordinary compass is to a ship at sea, that the vessel was a long way out of her course.

Such a thing had never yet occurred. Up to now the *Astronef* had obeyed the laws of gravitation and repulsion with absolute exactness. He made another examination of the instruments; but no, all were in perfect order.

"I wonder what the deuce is the matter," he said, after he had looked for a few moments with frowning eyes at the Heavens before him. "By Jove, we're swinging more. This is getting serious.

He went back to the compass. The long, slender needle was slowly swinging farther and farther out of the middle line of the vessel.

"There can only be two explanations of that," he went on, thrusting his hands deep into his trouser pockets; "either the engines are not working properly, or some enormous and invisible body is pulling us towards it out of our course. Let's have a look at the engines first."

When he reached the engine-room he said to Murgatroyd, who was indulging in his usual pastime of cleaning and polishing his beloved charges:

"Have you noticed anything wrong during the last hour or so, Murgatroyd?"

"No, my lord; at least not so far as concerns the engines. They're all right. Hark now, they're not making more noise than a lady's sewing machine," replied the old Yorkshireman with a note of resentment in his voice. The suspicion that anything could be wrong with his shining darlings was almost a personal offence to him. "But is anything the matter, my Lord, if I might ask?"

"We're a long way off our course, and for the life of me I can't understand it," replied Redgrave. "There's nothing about here to pull us out of our line. Of course the stars—good Lord, I never thought of that! Look here, Murgatroyd, not a word about this to her ladyship. and stand by to raise the power by degrees, as I signal to you."

"Ay, my lord. I hope it's nothing bad."

Redgrave went back to the conning-tower without replying. The only possible solution of the mystery of the deviation had suddenly dawned upon him, and a very serious solution it was. He remembered that there were such things as dead suns— the derelicts of the Ocean of Space— vast, invisible orbs, lightless and lifeless, too distant from any living sun to be illumined by its rays, and yet exercising the only force left to them— the force of attraction. Might not one of these have wandered near enough to the confines of the Solar system to exert this force, a force of absolutely unknown magnitude, upon the *Astronef*?

He went to a little desk beside the instrument-table and plunged into a maze of mathematics, of masses and weights, angles and distances. Half-an-hour later he stood looking at the last symbol on the last sheet of paper with something like fear. It was the fatal x which remained to satisfy the last equation, the unknown quantity which represented the unseen force that was dragging the *Astronef* into the outer wilderness of interstellar space, into far-off regions from which, with the remaining force at his disposal, no return would be possible.

He signalled to Murgatroyd to increase the development of the R. Force from a tenth to a half. Then he went to the lower saloon, where Zaidie was busy with her usual morning tidy-up. Now that the mystery was explained there was no reason to keep her in the

dark. Indeed, he had given her his word that he would conceal from her no danger, however great, that might threaten them when he had once assured himself of its existence.

She listened to him in silence and without a sign of fear beyond a little lifting of the eyelids and a little fading of the colour in her cheeks.

"And if we can't resist this force," she said, when he had finished, "it will drag us millions—perhaps millions of millions—of miles away from our own system into outer space, and we shall either fall on the surface of this dead sun and be reduced to a puff of lighted gas in an instant, or some other body will pull us away from it, and then another away from that, and so on, and we shall wander among the stars for ever and ever until the end of time!"

"If the first happens, darling, we shall die—together—without knowing it. It's the second that I'm most afraid of. The *Astronef* may go on wandering among the stars for ever—but we have only water enough for three weeks more. Now come into the conning-tower and we'll sec how things are going."

As they bent their heads over the instrument-table Redgrave saw that the remorseless needle had moved two degrees more to the right. The keel of the *Astronef*, under the impulse of the R. Force, was continually turning. The pull of the invisible orb was dragging the vessel slowly but irresistibly out of her line.

"There's nothing for it but this," said Redgrave, putting out his hand to the signal-board, and signalling to Murgatroyd to put the engines to their highest power. "You see, dear, our greatest danger is this; we have had to exert such a tremendous lot of power that we haven't any too much to spare, and if we have to spend it in counteracting the pull of this dead sun, or whatever it is, we may not have enough of what I call the R. fluid left to get home with."

"I see," she said, staring with wide-open eyes at the needle. "You mean that we may not have enough to keep us from falling into one of the planets or perhaps into the sun itself. Well, supposing the dangers are equal, this one is the nearest, and so I guess we've got to fight it first."

"Spoken like a good American!" he said, putting his arm across her shoulders and looking at once with infinite pride and infinite regret at the calm, proud face which the glory of resignation had adorned with a new beauty.

She bowed her head and then looked away again so that he should not see that there were tears in her eyes. He took his hand from her shoulder and stared in silence down at the needle. It was stationary again.

"We've stopped!" he said, after a pause of several moments. "Now, if the body that's taken us out of our course is moving away from us we win, if it's coming towards us we lose. At any rate, we've done all we can. Come along, Zaidie, let's go and have a walk on deck."

They had scarcely reached the upper deck when something happened which dwarfed all the other experiences of their marvellous voyage into utter insignificance.

Above and around them the constellations blazed with a splendour inconceivable to an observer on earth, but ahead of them gaped the vast, black void which sailors call "the coal-hole," and in which the most powerful telescopes have only discovered a few faintly luminous bodies. Suddenly, out of the midst of this infinity of darkness, there blazed a glare of almost intolerably brilliant radiance. Instantly the forward end of the *Astronef* was bathed in light and heat—the light and heat of a re-created sun, whose elements had been dark and cold for uncounted ages.

Hundreds of tiny points of light, unknown worlds which had been dark for myriads of years, twinkled out of the blackness. Then the fierce glare grew dimmer. A vast mantle of luminous mist spread out with inconceivable rapidity, and in the midst of this blazed the central nucleus—the sun which in far-off ages to come would be the giver of light and heat, of life and beauty to worlds unborn, to planets which were now only little eddies of atoms whirling in that ocean of nebulous flame.

For more than an hour the two voyagers stood motionless and silent, gazing on the indescribable splendours of a spectacle such as no human eyes but theirs had ever beheld. Every earthly thought seemed burnt out of their souls by the glory and the wonder of it. It was almost as though they were standing in the very presence of God, for were they not witnessing the supreme act of omnipotence, a new creation? Their peril, a peril such as had never threatened mortals before, was utterly forgotten. They had even forgotten each other's presence. For the time being they existed only to look and to wonder.

They were called at length out of their trance by the matter-of-fact voice of Murgatroyd saying: "My lord, she's back to her course. Will I keep the power on full?"

"My lord, she's back to her course. Will I keep the power on full?"

"Eh! What's that?" exclaimed Redgrave, as they both turned quickly round. "Oh, it's you, Murgatroyd. The power? Yes, keep it on full till I have taken the bearings."

"Ay, my lord, very good." replied the engineer.

As he left the deck Redgrave put his arm round Zaidie and drew her gently towards him and said: "Zaidie, truly you are favoured among women! You have seen the beginning of a new creation. You will certainly be saved somehow after that."

"Yes, and you too, dear," she murmured, as though still half-dreaming. "It is very glorious and wonderful; but what is it all—I mean, what is the explanation of it?"

"The merely scientific explanation, dear, is very simple. I see it all now. The force that was dragging us out of our course was the united pull of two dead stars approaching each other in the same orbit. They may have been doing that for millions of years. The shock of their meeting has transformed their motion into light and heat. They have united to form a single sun and a nebula, which will some day condense into a system of planets like ours. To-night the astronomers on earth will discover a new star—a variable star as they'll call it—for it will grow dimmer as it moves away from our system. It has often happened before."

Then they turned back to the conning-tower. The needle had swung to its old position. The new star, henceforth to be known in the annals of astronomy as Lilla-Zaidie, had already set for them to the right of the *Astronef* and risen on the left, and, at a distance of over nine hundred million miles from the earth, the corner was turned, and the homeward voyage began.

CHAPTER 20

A WEEK LATER they crossed the path of Jupiter, but the giant was invisible, far away on the other side of the sun. Redgrave laid his course so as to avail himself to the utmost of the "pull" of the planets without going near enough to them to be compelled to exert too much of the priceless R. Force, which the indicators showed to be running perilously low.

Between the orbits of Jupiter and Mars they made a decided economy by landing on Ceres, one of the largest of the asteroids, and travelling about fifty million miles on her towards the orbit of the earth without any expenditure of force whatever. They found the tiny world possessed of a breathable atmosphere and a fluid resembling water but nearly as dense as mercury. A couple of flasks of it form the greatest treasures of the British Museum and the National Museum at Washington. The vegetable world was represented by coarse grass, lichens, and dwarf shrubs, and the animal by different species of worms, lizards and flies, and small burrowing animals of the rodent type.

As the orbit of Ceres, like that of the other asteroids, is considerably inclined to that of the earth, the *Astronef* rose from its surface when the plane of the earth's revolution was reached, and the glittering swarm of miniature planets plunged away into space beneath them.

"Where to now?" said Zaidie, as her husband came down on deck from the conning-tower.

"I am going to try to steer a middle course between the orbits of Mercury and Venus," he replied. "They just happen to be so placed now that we ought to be able to get the advantage of the pull of both of them as we pass, and that will save us a lot of power. The only thing I'm afraid of is the pull of the sun, equal to goodness knows how many times the attraction of all the planets put together. You see, little woman, it's like this," he went on, taking out a pencil and going down on one knee on the deck: "Here's the *Astronef*; there's Venus; there's Mercury; there's the sun; and there, away on the other side of him, is Mother Earth: If we can turn that corner safely and without expending too much power we should be all right."

"And if we can't, what will happen?"

"It will be a choice between morphine and cremation in the atmosphere of the sun, dear, or rather gradually roasting as we fall towards it."

"Then, of course, it will be morphine," she said quite quietly, as she turned away from his diagram and looked at the now fast increasing disc of the sun. A well-balanced mind speedily becomes accustomed even to the most terrible perils, and Zaidie had now looked this one so long and so steadily in the face that for her it had already become merely the choice between two forms of death with just a chance of escape hidden in the closed hand of Fate.

Thirty-six earth-hours later the glorious golden disc of Venus lay broad and bright beneath them. Above was the blazing orb of the Sun, nearly half as big again as it appears from the earth, with Mercury, a round black spot, travelling slowly across it.

"My dear Bird-Folk!" said Zaidie, looking down at the lovely world below them. "If home wasn't home—"

"We can be back among them in a few hours with absolute safety," interrupted her husband, catching at the suggestion. "I've told you the truth about getting back to the earth. It's only a chance at best, and even if we pass the sun we may not have force enough left to prevent the *Astronef* from being smashed to dust or burnt up in the atmosphere. After all we might do worse—"

"What would you do if you were alone, Lenox?" she said, interrupting him in turn.

"I should take my chance and go on. After all home's home and worth a struggle. But you, dear—"

"I'm you, and so I take the same chances as you do. Besides, we're not perfect enough for a world where there isn't any sin. We should probably get quite miserable there. No, home's home, as you say."

"Then home it is, dear!" he replied.

The vast, resplendent hemisphere of the Love-Star sunk swiftly down into the vault of space, growing swiftly smaller and dimmer as the *Astronef* sped towards the little black spot on the face of the sun, which to them was like a buoy marking a place of utter and hopeless shipwreck in the ocean of immensity.

The chronometer, still set to Earth time, had now begun to mark the last hours of the *Astronef*'s voyage. She was not only travelling at a speed of which figures could give no comprehensible idea, but the Sun, Mercury, and the Earth were rushing towards her with a compound velocity, composed of the movement of the Solar System through space and of the movement of the two planets round the sun.

Murgatroyd was at his post in the engine-room. Redgrave and Zaidie had gone into the conning-tower, perhaps for the last time. For good fortune or evil, for life or death, they would see the end of the voyage together.

"How far yet, dear?" she said, as Venus began to slip away behind them, rising like a splendid moon in their wake.

"Only sixty million miles or so, a matter of a few hours, more or less— it all depends," he replied, without taking his eyes off the compass.

"Sixty millions! Why I feel almost at home again."

"But we have to turn the corner of the street yet, dear, and after that there's a fall of more than twenty-five million miles on to the more or less kindly breast of Mother Earth."

"A fall! It does sound rather awful when you put it that way; but I am not going to let you frighten me. I believe Mother Earth will receive her wandering children quite as kindly as they deserve."

The moon-like disc of Venus grew swiftly smaller, and the black spot on the face of the sun larger and larger as the *Astronef* rushed silently and imperceptibly, and yet with almost inconceivable velocity, towards doom or fortune. Neither Zaidie nor Redgrave spoke again for nearly three hours—hours which to them seemed to pass like so many minutes. Their eyes were fixed on the black disc of Mercury, which, as they approached it, expanded with magical rapidity till it completely eclipsed the blazing orb behind it. Their thoughts were far away on the still invisible Earth and all the splendid possibilities that it held for two young lives like theirs.

As the sunlight vanished they looked at each other in the golden moonlight of Venus, and Zaidie let her head rest for a moment on her husband's shoulder. Then a swiftly broadening gleam of light shot out from behind the black circle of Mercury. The first crisis had come. Redgrave put out his hand to the signal-board and rang for full power. The planet seemed to swing round as the *Astronef* rushed into the blaze. In a few minutes it passed through the phases from "new" to "full." Venus became eclipsed in turn as they swung between Mercury and the Sun, and then Redgrave, after a rapid glance to either side, said:

"If we can only keep the two pulls balanced we shall do it. That will keep us in a straight line, and our own momentum ought to carry us into the Earth's attraction."

Zaidie did not reply. She was shading her eyes with her hand from the almost intolerable brilliance of the sun's rays, and looking straight ahead to catch the first glimpse of the silver-grey orb. Her husband read her thoughts and respected them. But a few minutes later he startled her out of her dream of home by exclaiming:

"Good God, we're turning!"

"What do you say, dear? Turning what?"

"On our own centre. Look! I'm afraid only a miracle can save us now, darling."

She looked to the left-hand side where he was pointing. The sun, no longer now a sun, but a vast ocean of flame filling, nearly a third of the vault of space, was sinking beneath them. on the right Mercury was rising. Zaidie knew only too well what this meant. It meant that the keel of the *Astronef* was being dragged out of the straight line which would cut the earth's orbit some forty million miles away. It meant that, in spite of the exertion of the full power that the engines could develop, they had begun to fall into the sun.

Redgrave laid his hand on his wife's, and their eyes met. There was no need for words. Perhaps speech just then would have been impossible. In that mute glance each looked into the other's soul and was content. Then he left the conning-tower, and Zaidie dropped on to her knees before the instrument-table and laid her forehead upon her clasped hands.

Her husband went to the saloon, unlocked a little cupboard in the wall and took out a blue bottle of corrugated glass labeled "Morphine, Poison." He took another empty bottle of white glass and measured fifty drops into it. Then he went to the engine-room and said abruptly:

"Murgatroyd, I'm afraid it's all up with us. We're falling into the sun, and you know what that means. In a few hours the *Astronef* will be red-hot. So it's roasting alive—or this. I recommend this."

"And what might that be, my lord?" said the old engineer, looking at the bottle which his master held out towards him.

"That's morphine— poison. Fill that up with water, drink it, and in half-an-hour you'll be dead without knowing it. Of course, you won't take it until there's absolutely no hope; but, granted that, you'll find this a better death than roasting or baking alive." Then his voice changed suddenly as he went on: "Of course, I need not say, Murgatroyd, how deeply I regret now that I asked you to come in the *Astronef*."

"My lord, my people have served yours for seven hundred years, and, whether on earth or among the stars, where you go it is my duty to go also. But don't ask me to take the poison. It is not for me to say that a journey like this is tempting Providence, but, by my lights, if I am to die it will be the death that Providence in its wisdom sends."

"I daresay you're right in one way, Murgatroyd, but it's no time to argue about beliefs now. There's the bottle. Do as you think right. And now, in case the miracle doesn't happen, good-bye.

"Good-bye, my lord, if it be so," replied the old Yorkshireman, taking the hand which Redgrave held out to him. "I'll keep the power on to the last, I suppose?"

"Yes, you may as well. If it doesn't keep us away from the Sun it won't be much use to us in two or three hours."

He left the engine-room and went back to the conning-tower. Zaidie was still on her knees. Beneath and around them the awful gulf of flame was broadening and deepening. Mercury was rising higher and growing smaller. He put the bottle down on the table and waited. Then Zaidie looked up. Her eyes were clear, and her face was perfectly calm. She rose and put her arm through his, and said:

"Well, is there any hope, dear? There can't be now, can there? Is that the morphine?"

"Yes," he replied, slipping his arm beneath hers and round her waist. "I'm afraid there's not much hope now, little woman. We're using up the last of the power, and you see—"

As he said this he looked at the thermometer. The mercury had risen from 65 degrees Fahrenheit, the normal temperature of the interior of the *Astronef*, to 93 degrees, and during the half-minute that he watched it rose another degree. There was no mistaking such a warning as that. He had brought two little liqueur glasses in his pocket from the saloon. He divided the morphine between them, and filled them up with water.

"Not until the last moment, dear," said Zaidie, as he set one of them before her. "We have no right to do it until then."

"Very well. When the mercury reaches a hundred and fifty. After that it will go up ten and fifteen degrees at a jump, and we—"

"Yes, at a hundred and fifty," she replied, cutting short a speech she dared not hear the end of. "I understand. It will be impossible to hope any more."

Now, side by side, they stood and watched the thermometer.

Ninety-five—ninety-eight—a hundred and three—a hundred and ten—eighteen—twenty-four—thirty-two—forty-one.

The silent minutes passed, and with each the silver thread—for them the thread of life—grew, with strange contradiction, longer and longer, and with every minute it grew more quickly.

A hundred and forty-six.

With his right arm Redgrave drew Zaidie still closer to him. He put out his left hand and took up the little glass. She did the same.

"Good-bye, dear, till we have slept and wake again!"

"Good-bye, darling, God grant that we may!" But the agony of that last farewell was more than Zaidie could hear. She looked away at the little glass in her hand, a hand which even now did not tremble. Then she raised her eyes again to take one last look at the glory of the stars, and at the Fate incarnate in flame which lay beneath them.

"The Earth, the Earth—thank God, the Earth!"

With the hand that held the draught of Lethe—which in another moment would have passed her lips—she caught at her husband's hand, pulled the glass out of it, and then with a little sigh she dropped senseless on the floor of the conning-tower. Redgrave looked for a moment in the direction that her eyes had taken. A pale, silver-grey crescent, with a little white spot near it, was rising out of the blackness beyond the edge of the solar ocean of flame. Home was in sight at last, but would they reach it—and how?

He picked her up and carried her to their room and laid her on the bed. Then he went to the medicine chest again, this time for a very different purpose.

An hour later, they were on the upper deck with their telescopes turned on to the rapidly-growing crescent of the home-world, which, in its eternal march through space, had come into the line of direct attraction just in time to turn the scale in which the lives of the star-voyagers were trembling. The higher it rose, the bigger and broader and brighter it grew, and, at last, Zaidie—forgetting in her transport of joy all the perils that were yet to come—sprang to her feet and clapped her hands, and cried:

"There's America!"

Then she dropped back into her long deck-chair and began a good, hearty, healthy cry.

EPILOGUE

THERE IS LITTLE NOW to be told that all the world does not already know as well as it knows the circumstances of Lord and Lady Redgrave's departure from the Earth, at the beginning of that marvellous voyage, that desperate plunge into the unknown immensities of Space which began so happily, and yet with so many grave misgivings in the hearts of their friends, and which, after passing many perils, the adventurous voyagers finished even more happily than they had begun.

As I said at the beginning of this narrative the sole purpose of writing it has been to place before the reading public an account of the adventures experienced by Lord Redgrave and his beautiful Countess from the time of their departure from the Earth to the hour of their return to it. Therefore there is no need to re-tell a tale already told, and one that has been read and re-read a thousand times. Every one who has read his or her newspaper from Chamskatska to Cape Horn, and from Alaska to South Australia, knows how the Commander of the *Astronef* so nursed the remains which were left to him of the R. Force after overcoming the attraction of the Sun, that he was able to steer an oblique course between the Moon and the Earth, and to counteract what Zaidie called the all too-loving attraction of the Mother Planet, and, after sixty hours of agonising suspense, at last re-entered their native atmosphere.

The expenditure of the last few units of the R. Force enabled them to just clear the summits of the Bolivian Andes, to cross the foothills and western slopes of Peru, and finally to let the *Astronef* drop quietly on to the bosom of the broad Pacific about twenty miles westward of the Port of Mollendo.

All this time thousands of anxious eyes had been peering through telescopes every night in quest of the wanderers who must now be returning if ever they were to return, and a reward of ten thousand dollars, offered conjointly by the British and United States Governments for the first authentic tidings of the *Astronef*, was won by a smart young Californian, who was Assistant Astronomer at the Harvard University Observatory at Arequipa.

One night when he was on duty watching a lunar occultation, he saw something sweep across the disc of the full moon just as the captain and officers of the St. Louis had seen that same something sweep across the disc of the rising sun. What else could it be if not the *Astronef.* He rang for another assistant to go on with the occultation, and wired down to the coast requesting the British Consul at Mollendo to look out for an arrival from the skies.

Three hours later the gleam of an electric searchlight flickered down over the huge black cone of the Misti, and by dawn the next morning one of Her Majesty's cruisers—most appropriately named Astroea—attached to the Pacific Squadron then en route from Lima to Valparaiso, steamed out westward from Mollendo and found the long, shining hull of the *Astronef* waiting quietly on the unrippled rollers of the Pacific, and Lord and Lady Redgrave having breakfast in the deck-chamber.

Compliments and congratulations having been duly exchanged, she was taken in tow by the cruiser, and so reached Valparaiso. Here she lay for a few days while the wires of the world were being kept hot with telegraphic accounts of her return to Earth, and while her Commander, with the assistance of the officers of the National Laboratory, was replenishing his stock of the R. Fluid from the chemicals which they had placed at his disposal.

It would, of course, have been quite possible for him and Zaidie to have taken steamer northward to Panama, crossed the Isthmus, and returned to New York and Washington via Jamaica. The British Admiral even offered to place his fastest cruiser at their disposal for a run to San Francisco, whence the Overland Limited would have landed them in New York in four days and a half, but Zaidie vetoed this as quickly as she had done the other proposition. If she had her way the *Astronef* should go back to Washington as she had left it, by means of her own motive force, and so, of course, it came to pass.

Even Murgatroyd's grim and homely features seemed irradiated by a glow of what he afterwards thought unholy pride when he once more stood by his levers and heard the familiar signal coming from the conning-tower.

"A tenth."

And then— "Stand by steering-gear."

The next moment there was another tinkle in the engine-room.

Redgrave, standing with Zaidie in the conning-tower, moved the power-wheel through ten degrees, and then to the amazement of tens of thousands of spectators, the hull of the *Astronef* rose perpendicularly from the waters of the Bay. The British Squadron and a detachment of the Chilian fleet thundered out a salute which was answered a few moments later by the shore batteries, Redgrave went down into the deck-chamber and fired twenty-one shots from one of the Maxim-Nordenfelts—the same with which he had mown down the crowds of Martians in the square of their great city a hundred and thirty million miles away, and while he was doing this Zaidie in the conning-tower ran the White Ensign up to the top of the flagstaff.

Then the glass doors were closed again, the propellers began to revolve at their utmost speed, and the Space-Navigator with one tremendous leap cleared the double chain of the Andes and vanished to the north-eastward.

To describe the reception of Lord and Lady Redgrave when the *Astronef* dropped a few hours later, on to the very spot in front of the steps of the Capitol at Washington from which she had risen just four months before, would only be to repeat what has already been told in the Press of the world, and especially of the United States, with a far more luxuriant wealth of detail than could possibly be emulated here. Suffice it to say that the first human form that Zaidie embraced after her long wanderings was that of Mrs. Van Stuyler, whom the President of the United States had escorted to the gangway.

The most marvellous of human adventures become commonplace by repetition, and Mrs. Van Stuyler had already spent nearly a fortnight devouring every item, whether of fact or fancy, with which the American Press had embroidered the adventures of the *Astronef* and her crew. And so when the first embracings and emotions were over, all she could find to say was:

"Well, Zaidie dear, and how did you enjoy it, after all?"

"It was just gorgeous, Mrs. Van, and if there was a more gorgeous word than that in the American language I'd use it," replied Zaidie, with another hug, "Why didn't you come? You'd have been—well no, perhaps I'd better not say what you would have been. But just think of it, or try to—A honeymoon trip of over two thousand million miles, and back—safe—thank God!"

As she said this, Zaidie threw her arm over Mrs. Van Stuyler's shoulder, and drew her away towards the forward end of the deck-chamber. At the same moment the President's hand met Lord Redgrave's in a long, strong grip. They didn't say anything just then. Men seldom do under such circumstances.

THE END

The First Space Tourist ~ George Griffith

George Griffith would turn his formidable story-telling talents to space travel for a serial which ran in *Pearson's Magazine* from January to June 1900. It was called *Stories of Other Worlds* and the installment titles were, *A Visit to the Moon, The World of the War God, A Glimpse of the Sinless Star, The World of the Crystal Cities, In Saturn's Realm* and *Homeward Bound.* It is worth taking note of the date of publication, at least five months before H.G. Wells' *First Men in the Moon.* When Griffith was ready to send his protagonists out into space it would not be to merely visit the moon, his was a full-fledged expedition of space tourism. He later expanded the story and it was published by Pearson's as a novel in 1901 retitled "*A Honeymoon in Space.*"

In Griffith's major space epic he pulled together all of the familiar accouterments of his previous stories. Cigar-shaped airships, daring heroes, beautiful acquiescent heroines, outrageous battles and of course innovative technology. It is a long book for its time, over 300 pages, but in the details there is the usual display of creativity from Griffith. His trio of adventurers departs on a rip-roaring rush around the solar system in a hermetically sealed spacecraft that uses an undefined anti-gravity device for propulsion. Both the serial and the novel include evocative illustrations by Stanley Wood and Harold Piffard. The story takes place in November 1900, a mere 11 months after Griffith wrote it, so it is intended to be a near-future that his readers might conceivably recognize.

The novel includes a lengthy prologue that had been omitted from the serial. That prologue outlines the arrival of a wealthy English nobleman, Lord Redgrave, as he pulls his extraordinary airship alongside an ocean liner in mid-Atlantic. After chatting with the captain and crew of the liner he meets a previous acquiantance; the daughter of the airship's inventor. He then promptly whisks her away on an unforgettable voyage into space. Redgrave seals the ship and activates the air-scrubbers before heading out of the atmosphere. During the voyage he explains the effects of low gravity on his travelers before arriving at the moon in a mere 12 hours, where they alight at the crater Tycho. Having landed they pack their equipment for their exploration, which includes a "kodak" and a panoramic camera (something which the Apollo astronauts didn't take, but whose absence was compensated for by taking overlapping still images with a 70mm camera.) Once Lord Redgrave and his companion are ready to embark, they don pressure suits.

"The helmets were smaller (than diving helmets), and not having to withstand outside pressure they were made of welded aluminium, lined thickly with asbestos, not to keep the cold out but the heat in. On the back of the dress there was a square case, looking like a knapsack, containing the expanding apparatus, which would furnish breathable air for an almost unlimited time as long as the liquefied air from a cylinder hung below it passed through the cells in which the breathed air had been deprived of its carbonic acid gas and other noxious ingredients."

The exceptional description continues, *"The pressure of air inside the helmet automatically regulated the supply, which was not permitted to circulate through the other portions of the dress…any air in the dress, which was woven of a cunning compound of silk and asbestos, would instantly expand with irresistible force, burst the covering, and expose the limbs of the explorers to a cold which would be infinitely more destructive than the hottest of earthly fires."*

Griffith can surely be forgiven the inclusion of asbestos in his suit since he could hardly have been aware of the toxicity of the element. Once outside, the story continues with this uncanny portrayal of the surroundings and equipment, *"They were in the shade cast by the hull of the* Astronef. *For about ten yards in front of her was a dense shadow, and beyond it a stretch of grey-white sand lit by a glare of sunlight which would have been intolerable if it had not been for the smoke-colored slips of glass which had been fitted behind the glass visors of the helmets."*

The adventurers see the ruins of an ancient city and Redgrave speculates that the inhabitants may have been driven underground, an idea dating back to Bernard De Fontenelle that H.G. Wells would embellish in his own lunar story later that year. Redgrave and his companion investigate the possibility of an atmosphere by striking a match to no avail, a trick employed 29 years later by Fritz Lang in his movie *Frau Im Mond.* They then descend into the depths of Newton crater and Griffith's prose is eerily reminiscent of the Millenium Falcon flying into the maw of an enormous asteroid in George Lucas' *Empire Strikes Back.* The Astronef switches on its searchlights and soon settles deep inside the moon where they discover water and an atmosphere. After a disturbing encounter with the local sub-selenian fauna they depart and head for Mars.

The Martians are still living on an old and decaying planet. Earthly astronomers had not yet shifted their opinion about the natural course of a planet's life and continued to labour under the misapprehension that all planets go through a life course ultimately ending up in senescence and decay. Griffith then mentions Camille Flammarion's story *Omega The End of the World*, a clear sign that he was aware of it and had probably been influenced by the great astronomer.

Next, Redgrave flies his *Astronef* into the Martian atmosphere where he encounters a large fleet of Martian warships. The Martians open fire using shells armed with chemical warheads, but the airtight ship protects its daring entourage. Redgrave engages the enemy by ramming a Martian vessel. The accompanying illustration in the book is one of the first pictures to show a space battle. The Martians are caught off guard and *"human figures more than half as large again as men were staring at them through the windows in the sides…in a second the Astronef's spur pierced her, the Martian ship broke in twain, and her two halves plunged downwards through the rosy clouds."*

The Martian ships are portrayed in Stanley Wood's picture as a sort of cigar-shaped metal tube with masts and portholes. Accompanied by Griffith's description of the Martians peering from the portholes, you are left with the distinct impression you have just met a full-fledged archetype of a UFO.

After beating the Martians, quite convincingly, the *Astronef* heads to Venus. In Griffith's universe it is a beautiful pristine world of snow-covered mountains and silver mists. It is populated by winged humanoids that Griffith refers to as angel-like. They are apparently capable of flight due to the fact they have four wings and a tail for steering and they are supported by an atmosphere two and a half times denser than earth's. Almost certainly this version of Venus lingered on into the works of later scribes such as C.S. Lewis and others. Ultimately the Venusian encounter is uneventful and so the spacecraft embarks for Jupiter.

Another completely remarkable sojourn takes place when the ship diverts to Jupiter's moon, Callisto.

"In another hour or so the Astronef had dropped gently onto the surface of Callisto at the foot of a range of mountains crowded with jagged and splintery peaks, and a mile or two away from the edge of a sea of snow and ice which stretched away in a vast expanse of rugged frozen billows beyond the horizon.

"After this they went and put on their breathing dresses and went for a welcome stroll along the arid shores of the frozen sea after their lengthy confinement to the decks of the Astronef."

A lucky guess by Griffith? Certainly the telescopes of his time may well have detected a bright surface on Callisto and the astronomers deduced a sea of ice but it would be almost a century later before the Voyager probes would confirm the frozen surface of some of Jupiter's satellites. He even explains how Ganymede has an aurora, and he could scarcely have had any inkling of Jupiter's intense radiation belt which does indeed suggest that such aurora can exist. In this story, Ganymede is populated by a humanoid species who live indoors in glass cities. Griffith describes a series of variable speed roadways that run in parallel throughout the cities. Moving walkways that would become a staple of science fiction until becoming reality many years later. After some interaction with the Ganymedian population he notes from on high that Europa has declined into its final stage and is in the "icy silence of death."

Next Redgrave flies the Astronef into the Jovian atmosphere to take a peek at what lies beneath the clouds. Griffith goes along with astronomer Richard Proctor's version of the giant planet, describing an infernal and hellish surface of lava and flame constantly remaking itself and completely hostile to life. Later he confirms his familiarity with Proctor when they move on to Saturn and the hero, Redgrave, discusses how the rings need to be navigated with caution because of, *"...Proctor's hypothesis that the rings are formed of multitudes of tiny satellites."* He continues, *"Those are rings of what we should call meteorites on Earth, atoms of matter which Saturn threw off into space after the satellites were formed."*

At last the Astronef turns for home and during the voyage Redgrave demonstrates to his fiancée the benefits of zero gravity. *"Stooping down and taking hold of the chair with both hands, without any apparent effort he raised her about five feet from the floor, and held her there...for a moment he let her go, and she and the chair floated between the roof and the floor."*

This description makes it quite clear that some of the implications of zero gravity were well understood by the turn of the century. After turning for home the Astronef is subjected to one last hazard while en route. An invisible gravitational anomaly that Griffith calls, *"A derelict of the Ocean of Space, vast invisible orbs, lightless and lifeless, too distant from any living sun to be illumined by its rays, and yet exercising the only force left to them—the force of attraction."*

It's not exactly a black hole but it is close kin, and for the time of writing, 1900, it was absolutely cutting edge. The dark star manages to pull the ship far enough off course that Redgrave is obliged to rethink his trajectory. He decides to fly in towards the sun and use Venus and Mercury to provide gravitational boosts to slingshot the Astronef back on course and on to Earth where he splashes down in the Pacific. This has to be Griffith's tour de force. It is so far beyond anything else in fiction at the time that it really does beggar parallel. About the only person writing such stories, with such conviction and intelligence, was Russian rocket pioneer Konstantin Tsiolkovsky, but Griffith was certainly unaware of his work.

While H.G. Wells' great space epic of travel to the moon would be a deliberate reversion to Lucianic satire and would not begin to appear in serial form until four months after Griffith was done touring the entire solar system, Griffith's was a tour de force of imaginative technology and adventure.

H.G. Wells would admit a grudging fascination with his competitor although he would write an unfavorable review of Griffith in the *Saturday Review* in 1895. He would later mention Griffith in his book *The War in the Air* in which he described Griffith's *Outlaws of the Air* as an "aeronautic masterpiece."

George Griffith is a forgotten titan of his era. Part of the fault for this undoubtedly rests in the fact that his publisher,

Tower of London, went bankrupt in June of 1896. By October of that year Griffith found himself in court in London trying to stop the liquidators from selling off the copyrights. Ultimately he won the battle (and set a legal precedent doing so) but it must have been costly and time consuming and in the meantime it left him with no publisher for his most successful early works, the two Romanoff novels and *Outlaws of the Air*. He died on June 4th 1906.

Robert Godwin
(Burlington May 2011)